Charley

Charley

by
Donna Marie Seim

Illustrated by Susan Spellman

Donna Marie Seim

PETER E. RANDALL PUBLISHER
PORTSMOUTH, NEW HAMPSHIRE
2013
UPNE

ISBN: 978-1-937721-10-7
Library of Congress Control Number: 2013935546

Published by
Peter E. Randall Publisher
Box 4726
Portsmouth, NH 03802
www.perpublisher.com

Book design: Faith Hague

University Press of New England

For Russell,
my friend and superb story teller.

And to Troon Harrison,
my writing guardian angel.

Advance praise from readers of *Charley*

—⟶═○ ○═⟵—

"Basing her supremely delightful story upon real events and places, Donna Seim captures the world of orphans and foster children of early twentieth-century America. It is hard to not fall in love with Charley, the foster child from the city streets of Boston, who finds himself living with a foster family on a farm in Maine. How Charley adjusts to his world, given his own personal tragedy, is a story of courage and resilience. This is a must read for all children trying to envision the past and understand a world that no longer exists but which gave rise to the present. An excellent history primer." **—Lawrence J. Yerdon, President and CEO, Strawbery Banke Museum**

"Although Charley's world of city orphanages and dairy farming recalls a bygone era, the message at the heart of Donna Seim's poignant novel is timeless. Through the eyes of an orphaned child, Seim explores the struggles and triumphs faced by countless 'little wanderers' as they attempt to make sense of their pasts and build new lives, often in the care of families whose circumstances are radically different from those of their previous upbringings. Writing with empathy for the practical challenges and ambivalent feelings experienced by everyone involved in foster placements, Seim nevertheless conveys an unwavering faith in the belief that no matter how unconventional their path, every child deserves a loving family."

—Joan Wallace-Benjamin, President & CEO, The Home for Little Wanderers

"This is a great story!"

—Gabe, age 12

"Our entire class was riveted to your story...we were sad to have it over."

"Donna used great descriptive vocabulary, lots of 'juicy' words! I felt like I was there especially during the fire."

"We loved the character of Charley, his flaws, his courage and tenderness."

—**Students from the 2nd-4th multi-grade classroom, River Valley Charter School, Newburyport, MA**

"In this wonderful, well-written book of the same name, a twelve year old boy named Charley discovers the gifts within his experiences with family, friends, teachers, and others along the way that shape his growing up, and his future.

Today's young reader, boy or girl, is likely to be amazed at the chores required of Charley, whether it's collecting eggs from Bertha the hen, milking "the ladies," cutting ice on the pond, or stacking hay in the barn. The author has created moments of suspense for the reader to contemplate; they may know what they want to have happen to Charley next, hoping for success when it seems unlikely, but along the way they will never be quite sure how Charley's story will end.

Many of us have loved following along life's road with fictional characters like Huck Finn. Here we can cherish the fictionalized story of real characters in a world our grandparents and great grandparents often just hinted at. Was it really like that back then, at times that difficult? Early 20th century American life in both the city and country come alive for the reader.

I loved *Charley*. Seim provides us with a powerful reality of family and struggles, but with an abundance of hope, and an appreciation for the resilience of one young person's life."

—**Marjorie Lynn, Editor of a memoir *Boys Will Be Men: A Son Comes of Age In His Own Words*, and *Shore Lines: Life Lessons From The Sea***

Contents

Preface

CHARLEY'S STORY is set in the year of 1910. It was a time of massive immigration of European people into the United States. One of the huge waves of immigration was the Irish, fleeing from starvation, oppression, and poverty; they crossed the Atlantic Ocean in hopes of a better life. Unfortunately, they were unprepared to cope with the big cities teaming with immigrants like themselves. As each wave arrived they became the underdog, finding it hard to carve out a place in this new land called America. Many never made it past the big cities; men, women and older children found themselves working in factories for long hours under horrible conditions for pennies a day.

With both parents working long hours—twelve hours a day would not be unusual—the younger school-aged children, with more freedom than what was good for them, were often uncared and unaccounted for. They skipped school, pitched pennies, sold newspapers on street corners, and got into trouble with the law for stealing food. Truant officers arrested the ones who were not attending school, or were found pitching pennies on a Sunday morning. The child offender would be taken to court and have to appear before a judge; from there they would often be sentenced to a house of detention, which is like a jail for children.

It became such a daunting social problem that during the late 1800s and early 1900s many orphanages, some not so reputable, sprang up to care for the homeless children. One well-known and highly held one still in existence today is the Home for Little Wanderers, formerly called the New England Home for Little Wanderers. Hundreds of children walked through their doors every year. The mission of the Home was not to provide a long-term institutional home for these children, but rather a temporary place to give them shelter, food, clothing, health care and to teach them good manners. Once the child was deemed ready, they would be placed in a good upstanding "Christian" family as soon as possible. One very successful way of placing children was the practice of lining them up after a church service and having families pick children to take home with them.

Due to the rise in crime and rampant diseases; such as diphtheria, cholera, tuberculosis, small pox, and many others; it was believed cities were not healthy environments for children to grow up in. It was thought that farms and country living provided a much more wholesome setting for children. As a result, trains became a regular means to transport children from eastern cities, like Boston and New York, to the Midwest and rural New England states. Farming families were eager to pick boys to help with the never-ending farm work. Girls, much harder to place, became nannies or household help. Some children were unhappy and ran away, many stayed with the family until they came of age. Some were luckier than others by landing in good families. Few were adopted. Adoption was rare due to the fact that if the parents did not sign a release, even if they themselves could not care for the child or were totally absent, the child could not be adopted.

Today orphanages are not as prevalent as they were in Charley's time. However, there are many thousands of children all over the world, including the United States, in need of homes and families. Charley's story portrays the universal truth that every child inherently needs a loving home and family.

CHAPTER 1

The Donut Heist

"Okay, Big Dan! Up!" Charley stood balanced on Big Dan's broad shoulders. Dan rose from a squatting position to his full height. Charley reached up, his fingertips danced on the cracks in the brick wall.

"Give me a couple a inches and we will be rollin' in the dough!" Charley strained to stretch his arms higher. He made his wiry body rigid as Big Dan grabbed his ankles and boosted him upwards another half a foot. Charley gripped the framework of the window and in a split second he was through the opening, the worn soles of his shoes disappearing into the black slit.

Charley landed spread-eagle on a wooden counter lined with loaves of day old bread. He scrambled to his feet, inhaling the sweet nutty smell of fresh baked goods. His tongue lolled about in his mouth like a wet sponge as he ogled racks loaded with crusty breads and buttery rolls. He had to act fast! Morelli could show up at any time. He made a few frenzied selections and stacked them near the window. His eyes darted back and forth across fields of honey-glazed and sugar-dusted doughnuts. Charley could not ignore the growling bear in his stomach any longer. He couldn't remember when he had eaten last. Was it yesterday? He jammed a jelly doughnut into his mouth. The melting crust of sugar and dough exploded into heavenly sweetness as raspberry jam drizzled down his chin. Delirious with pleasure he stacked up a towering pile of a dozen assorted doughnuts. Then he spotted the pies! They were filled to the brim with tart red cherries and cinnamon-covered apples beneath crisscrossed pastry tops. The smells made him dizzy. He slid a cherry pie from the rack.

He could hear the guys outside. They'd been pitchin' coppers in the alley, but now they were getting antsy. "Hey, Charley baby, you gonna share some of that sweet dough wit us?" Chip, tall and lanky, was the boss of the gang. Tougher than any of the others, he gave the orders and he would take the biggest chunk of the haul. Charley climbed back up on the counter. He heaved two loaves of bread out the window followed by a barrage of dinner rolls.

"Charley, we's waitin' for the do'nuts! We know you's stuffin' yous self wit' all dem gooey goodies." That was

Skinny, always sour and wanting more than his fair share. Charley, feeling feisty, thought he'd have himself a little fun. He winged the doughnuts out the window, just high enough to make the boys dance for them. This was his one chance to be top dog. Once he climbed back through the window he would be the shortest member of the gang. Chip always picked him to crawl through the window and that made Charley feel important.

The resounding bang of a door slamming sent an electric shock rocketing to Charley's brain.

"Shoot! I'm outta here!" Charley grabbed the pie and lobbed it out the window. He aimed for Big Dan's enormous hands. Dan, not being ready to catch a spring-loaded pie, ducked. It sailed over his head, only to be stopped short by the alley wall behind him. Cherries the color of blood stuck together in a clump and then slithered down the craggy cement in a sticky mess. Next came Charley. He catapulted out the window, landing on a frazzled Big Dan. Dan, stunned, fell backwards with Charley on top of him, landing square on the remains of the cherry pie.

"Stoppa! Thievesa! Policea! Policea! Stoppa dem!" A flour-covered face with bulging eyes peered through the half-open window at the boys down below.

"Git goin'! It's old man Morelli!" yelped Charley as he pulled himself to his feet. Chip disappeared over the alley wall; Skinny took a sharp left and in a flash was out of sight. Charley charged down the alley with Big Dan loping behind.

"Man, we get caught they'll throw us in the house of detention." Big Dan puffed, holding onto two squished doughnuts and a deflated loaf of bread, his pockets bulging with dinner rolls. "Why didn't ya tell me ya was gonna throw me a pie?"

"Sorry, Dan, didn't have time, I heard old man Morelli bang the door. I had ta get out quick!" Charley slowed his pace, allowing Dan to catch up before turning the corner onto Boston's busy Tremont Street. "Don't ya worry a bit; Morelli ain't catchin' us! He's so full of his own dough, he couldn't run more'n a few feet without croakin'."

A trolley clanged by, wheels squealing on the metal rails imbedded in the street. Charley leapt onto the back step of the car, grabbing hold of the railing with one hand. Dan clomped on the bottom step beside Charley. The streetcar sped down the street. The two boys jumped off the car as it hissed to a stop. A disgruntled conductor shook his fist at them as they disappeared around the corner. They slowed their pace as they walked past sweet smelling crates of fruits and vegetables piled high in front of a neighborhood grocery store. Charley picked out a ripe peach and slid it into his pocket. Ah, this was Salem Street, his favorite street of the whole North End of Boston. They sauntered past a butcher shop displaying headless chickens, skinned rib cages of cows, and rabbit carcasses hung in the window. A red and white spiral pole spun round and round announcing the neighborhood barbershop. Men sat reading newspapers waiting for a haircut and whisker trim. Charley retrieved the peach out of his pocket and bit a chunk out of it. Then handing it to Dan said, "Here, take the rest."

"If that flatfoot Houlihan comes nosing around here we're dead meat." Sweat poured down Big Dan's red cheeks. His cap of fuzzy hair shone bright orange in the late summer sun. Dan chomped down on the peach like a starved rhinoceros, juice slid down the sides of his mouth and chin. He spit the pit onto the cobblestone road.

"The clock in the Boston Commons ain't rung five times yet; we won't see no Houlihan till then." Charley flipped his cap backwards and walked with his feet splayed outwards like a duck. He swung a make-believe billy club at his side and pointed his nose upright in the air. Big Dan leaned against the iron fence holding onto his belly and gasped for breath.

"Charley, you sure kin make me laugh!"

"Catch your breath and we'll divvy up what's left of the loot." Charley took off his cap and pushed back his ink black curls. Whenever he broke a sweat his hair turned into thick corkscrews. He had a habit of parting it down the middle and tucking it under his cap.

Dan cut Charley his share: a half loaf of bread, a couple of rolls and what was once a doughnut. Charley handed the rolls and doughnut back to Dan. "Go ahead, you take 'em. You're the oldest, and you got all of your sisters and mom to feed. I'm lucky. I got Pa and George."

"Thanks Charley! But next time will ya let me know you's gonna throw me a pie?"

Charley tapped his cap and smiled. "See ya tomorrow, big buddy; maybe we'll pitch us some coppers down by the wharf." Then, as the clock chimed five, he tucked his battered loaf of bread under his arm and headed for home whistling, "Oh Danny boy, the pipes, the pipes are calling, from glen to glen and down the mountain side . . ." His belly felt good with the doughnut and peach filling it up a little. And maybe Pa would be comin' home with some good grub. It was Friday after all, and maybe, if they were lucky, it was payday!

CHAPTER 2

The Letter

"Hey, George, I'm home!" Charley puffed as he opened the door, catching his breath from running the full five flights of stairs to the top of the tenement house. Charley placed the broken bread on the table, next to a white envelope.

"Where you been, Charley boy? Stayin' outta trouble?" George reclined in the chair their pa always sat on. He held a cigar between his thumb and index finger. George brought it slowly to his mouth and inhaled deeply, closing his eyes. As he exhaled, a cloud of white smoke filled the room. Charley couldn't stand the stink of cigar. The smoke made his eyes water and his throat scratchy.

"George, why you gotta smoke that thing? It's disgustin'!" Charley waved the air with his hand trying to disperse the smoke.

"I got something to tell you, Charley. It's important." George put the cigar down on a half filled ashtray. Smoke continued to curl upwards. Charley wanted to open a window to get some fresh air, but there was no window to open. It made him feel trapped. The space they rented from old man Snodgrass was more like a closet than a room. The only furnishings were a gas lamp, a battered old table, a couple of chairs and the coverless mattresses stacked in the corner.

"What's so important? Is Dad coming home tonight? And where is Minnie? A six-year-old girl should be home before dark." Charley didn't want to hear any bad news and for some reason—maybe it was the way George smoked the cigar—he was feeling bad news was coming his way.

"Minnie is playing with the Kilbane kids downstairs and Clarence is with her; the missus is feedin' them some warm potato soup. She don't have enough to feed her own kids, but Clarence and Minnie are so pitiful skinny she feels sorry for them. Charley, it's Pa that I want to talk to you about." His grey green eyes had a sad look to them. Charley winced, George was only fourteen and he looked like an old man.

"What about Pa? Did he get a job? Did he go back to the streetcar? We weren't so bad off when he was a streetcar conductor." Charley tapped his foot restlessly on the floor.

"No, that's just it; Pa didn't get a job. You know he hasn't been able to keep a job for more than a week or two since Ma and Sammy died. He just sings at the pub and they pay him with beer and a little grub. That's what he brings home, Charley, stale leftover food nobody else wants except the rats. I got my job at the factory, but a stinkin' forty cents a day ain't enough to keep me alive, let alone four of us. Figure it out, Charley; it's ten cents a day for each of us."

"Why doesn't Pa care about us anymore? He has to get a job. In just a couple a years I'll be fourteen. I can quit school and get a job at the candy factory. Shoot! We'll be rollin' in the dough. Maybe we can even get a room with a sink in it and a toilet down the hall!" Charley could feel his Irish temper spiraling like the smoke from the cigar.

"We have to face facts, Charley boy. Besides, this is what I got to tell you; Pa is gone." George's cheeks burned pink as he picked up the cigar and prepared for another deep inhale.

"That's crazy! Pa wouldn't leave us, even if he couldn't take care of us! You're lying, George! Why would you lie like that? I don't believe you!" Charley punched the air like a boxer with clenched fists. One swing clipped the cigar out of George's hand. It hit the table and landed on the corner of the white envelope. George jumped from his seat, his hand reached out to save his cigar. There on the white envelope were the beginnings of a smoldering brown burn. Charley pinched the end of the envelope and let it drop to the floor. He stomped his foot on the burnt edge over and over again as if he were trying to kill it.

"Charley, get a hold of yourself! It's not on fire!" George bent over from his chair and picked up the envelope. "This is a letter from Pa. He says he's going out West to find work. He will send for us when he does. In the meantime, he wants you and Minnie and Clarence to go to the New England Home for Little Wanderers. They'll take care of you and teach you some good manners. They'll find you a home and a family. I can't do it by myself Charley! You have to try to understand."

"Ya, I understand. We're like orphans! No one wants us. Not even our own pa. Not even you, George!"

"Can't you get it through your thick skull! I can't make the rent, Charley. We're three months behind; old man Snodgrass said he was coming tomorrow to collect it. He says if I don't pay him he is gonna kick us out. I just don't got the six bucks to pay him." George took the stub of the cigar and jammed it in the ashtray. "I'm going to bunk with a couple of the guys I work with down by the wharf. There'll be six of us men sleeping in the same room. No heat in the winter and stinkin' hot in the summer. It's no place for children."

"Well I ain't goin' to no home for no wanderers! Minnie and Clarence can go, but I'm stayin' with you. I can quit school. Don't go anyways. I can get a paper route; I'll beg if I have to. I'm almost twelve. I'm too old to go to an orphanage. We'll be okay together, George; we'll be okay."

George's gray green eyes met Charley's blue ones. "I need you to go to the Home, too. It will make it easier for Minnie and Clarence if you go with them. You three will be together, and they won't feel so abandoned that way. I'll keep track of you guys; I promise you that. Just think, you'll have a decent bed to sleep in and good food to eat."

"I ain't going!"

"No more stealing bread, Charley!"

"I ain't going!"

⋆⇒ CHAPTER 3 ⇐⋆

A Home for Wanderers

Charley placed one foot and then the other on the granite step. Facing him, only three short steps away, hung the huge mahogany doors of the orphanage. He felt Minnie's small cold hand tucked in his. Her hair was bedraggled and knotted in the back like a rat's nest. Her coat was dirty and frayed at the edges. It was at least two sizes too small. Green goo was running from her nose down her face. He yearned to wipe it, but he didn't have a rag and didn't want to sacrifice his own sleeve. Her thin cotton dress hung down long under her coat. Brown, stained stockings, refusing to cling to her skinny legs, slid downward in limp puddles around her ankles. She turned her face up to him and smiled, her brown eyes shining. Charley was taken aback. She didn't look scared. Instead she looked as if she were going to a birthday party.

George raced up the three granite steps and grasped onto the doorknob of the towering door. Charley groaned. Once that big door swung shut behind him, his life would never be the same again. Resentment and anger churned and gurgled with the crusts of bread in his stomach. It was just last night that George talked him into this whole thing. He had laid the guilt on heavy about Minnie and Clarence. "Girls can't make it on the street like boys can.

If they are lucky they become scullery maids, scrubbing someone's big house and taking care of seven brawling brats at the same time, but that is only if they are lucky." George had a somber look on his face that Charley wished away. "And Clarence is only eight; he'd have a better chance in life if he got a good family. And you too, Charley, a much better chance in life than workin' in a stinkin' cold and thankless factory for the rest of it!" His brother's words ran circles in Charley's head. He wanted to erase them, chop them up with his penknife and make them disappear. But they were indelibly scribbled in his memory to haunt him. He couldn't let Clarence and Minnie down. There was nothing to do but go up the stairs and through the door.

The foursome walked timidly into the front foyer of the hulking red brick building. The floors were polished to such a bright shine that when Charley looked down he saw his own image reflected back at him. It made him feel, for certain, that they did not belong here. Charley glanced down the long hallway lined with tall windowless doors on either side. It wasn't anything like he had imagined a home would look like. To top it off, there was not one kid in sight.

"I gotta pee, Charley! I really gotta!" Minnie looked up at him pulling on his arm. "I ain't kiddin'—it's gonna come down my leg, right now!"

"Hold on! How am I supposed to know where the can is?" Charley's protective feeling vanished. He wished she were holding onto George instead of him. Just then a door opened and a woman marched towards them. Her eyes seared through Charley then moved to Clarence, Minnie and George as she appraised them. Her boney nose rose high in the air while the thin line of her lips was set deep with disapproval.

"Good morning. Do you have an appointment?" Her frosty words pierced the silence.

"Excuse me, ma'am, my name is George Kimball Ryan and these are my two brothers, Clarence and Charley, and my sister, Minnie. Our mother passed away two years ago and our father has gone out West to find work. He left this here letter. He gives his permission for the kids to come here, to the Wanderers Home. He says it's a good place for them to be. It's all in the letter." George handed the envelope to the lady. He avoided her stern countenance by inspecting the broken fingernails of his left hand. She took the partially browned envelope with her lace hanky and pinched a pair of spectacles on the end of her nose. She read the letter, sniffed, and said, "Take off your caps and follow me."

They paraded in single file after her. George went first, then Minnie, followed by Clarence and Charley. Charley's foot slipped, causing him to look down. There on the floor was a river of yellow water. Oh Lord! That awful woman scared the pee right out of Minnie. Minnie kept walking not missing a step or looking back. Charley's attention was next drawn to Clarence walking beside him. Clarence had rolled his cap up and was wringing the life out of it. His blonde curls stuck plastered to his pale forehead while a few patches charged with static electricity jutted out in wild tufts.

"You must first meet Reverend Matthews, the director of the Home. I will give him this letter. You will remain silent unless he asks you a question. Do you understand?" She snapped the glasses off her nose and looked down at the children. All four bobbed their heads in unison. She opened a large door and motioned that they should go in.

Reverend Matthews was a slender man in his late forties. He looked stern with his fuzzy sideburns and thick black beard on his chin. His top lip was completely clean-shaven. He rose from his desk as the children entered. "Well! Who do we have here, Mistress Cummings?" He spoke directing his attention to the children.

"They just arrived. Here is the letter from their father. It seems he has abandoned them. And the mother is dead. They are half orphans." She patted her hair as if to tame a stray strand. But there were no loose hairs that Charley could see. They were all pulled back into a shiny black knob at the back of her head. The words she had just callously used—"abandoned," "mother dead" and "half orphans"—ricocheted in his ears. His stomach contracted in heaving waves of rebellion. "Oh no," he thought, "throwing up right now would be worse than Minnie's leakin' on the floor." Charley held on, clenching his fists till his knuckles turned white and his fingernails left deep imprints in his palms.

After reading the letter, Reverend Matthews reclined in his chair and folded his hands on his desk. He addressed the group, looking at each one as he spoke. "Your father has written a kind letter which shows his concern for your welfare. We are here to help children who do not have proper Christian homes. Your father was wise to write this letter because without his permission we would be of no service to you. You see, if one parent is still alive, as in your case, we need the consent of that parent before we can place you in a good and caring home. Now, before we start the procedures for your acceptance into the Home, do you have any questions?"

George, his cheeks a dullish red, spoke up. "Sir, will they be placed with the same family? I plan on keeping in touch with them, and I'd like to have knowledge of the fact that they will be together." George exhaled the last words like he was puffing out the smoke of his cigar.

Reverend Matthews raised his dark bushy eyebrows. He cleared his throat as if he needed more time before he answered, then said, "Well, George, my boy, we will do everything under God's great heavens to make sure your sister and brothers stay together. That is our policy! We keep our siblings together, whenever we can." The reverend lifted a watch out of his vest pocket that was attached by a gold chain. "Mistress Cummings, I think it is time to welcome our new house members." He smiled in a grand-fatherly manner and said, "George, you stay here with me, you can help me fill out all the paperwork."

Mistress Cummings commanded, "Come with me, children."

Minnie ran to George and threw her arms around him crying, "George! I don't want to go! Please, don't make me live here. I'll miss you too much." George hugged Minnie back and kissed her forehead. "Now go with the lady; I will come visit you, I promise. This is for the best; this is what Pa wanted." George peeled Minnie off of himself and placed her between Charley and Clarence. Then he sat down across from the reverend. "Okay, sir, I am ready to do the papers."

Mistress Cummings swept past Charley, Clarence and Minnie without touching them and guided them back out into the hallway. Without a word she ushered them into an empty room down the hall. Once the door was closed, she spun around and said, "First, Minnie, we will send you up to the nurse to be checked for lice. You will need to have your hair cut. It is a disgrace! If you have lice you will have to be treated and kept separate from the other children. The doctor will check you for any communicable diseases. Your nose is running. Do you have a bad cough? Never mind, the doctor will know. If you have tuberculosis you will not be allowed to stay here."

Minnie started to whimper. She ran to Charley and buried her head deep into his jacket. "I don't want them to cut my hair, Charley; please don't let them."

Charley, feeling helpless, tried to comfort her. "Don't worry, Minnie, I won't leave you alone."

"Oh no! The boys are separated from the girls! You may see each other at mealtimes or on the playground, but the girls live in their own wing on this side of the house and the boys live on the other."

Minnie dove into Charley's jacket once again and shook her head in defiance. "I won't go by myself, Charley.

I want to go home!" Charley detached her from himself and whispered, "You must be a brave girl for me and go with the nurse. It will just be a short while. I will find you and we will see each other every day." He felt his protectiveness resurfacing with a vengeance, and then he noticed that the green slime from her nose was gone.

Mistress Cummings continued giving orders, ignoring Minnie's display. "After you go through the medicals, you will be bathed. All children bathe once a week here. Cleanliness is next to godliness. Next we can move on to the seamstress. She will measure you and outfit you in brand new, proper clothes. This takes some time, so in the meanwhile you will be given some temporary clothing. Your present clothing and any possessions you have will be burned, of course." Charley's blood froze. Burned? His clothes? His things burned? His hand slipped into his coat pocket fingering its contents. No one, no way, was going to take this away from him!

Clarence raised his hand as if he were in a classroom waiting his turn to ask the teacher a question, "Um, ma'am, um, when do we get to eat?"

CHAPTER 4

Knife, Fork and Spoon

"Empty your pockets and place everything you have in one of these three boxes." Charley squeezed the comb in his hand, trying to shove it up the arm of his coat. Mistress Cummings glared at him. "No use trying to hide anything, young man; this is for your own good. Your possessions will be safe here. When you are placed into a family, the box with all its contents will be given back to you."

Charley cussed under his breath; it was no use—this lady was a jail warden! He winced as Clarence placed his meager possessions into one of the boxes: a bent nail, a flattened penny and two cats-eye marbles. Minnie dug deep in her coat pocket and pulled out a homemade clothespin doll. She kissed it and looked up pleadingly. "Her name is Millie; she is my best friend. Please, may I keep her?" Tears welled up in her eyes, giving them a feverish glow. "My mama made her for me."

"No Minnie, do as you are told. The clothespin will be saved for you. If you take it with you, it will be burned with your clothes; that is your choice."

Minnie laid the doll down into her box and patted her as she whimpered, "Tu-ra-lur-a-lur-a, hush now, don't you cry." Charley squeezed her shoulder gently with his right hand.

Charley's left hand was still frozen in his pocket. Sweat soaked his shirt. His brain told his hand to pull the comb out of his pocket but his muscles would not obey. "What is it you have in your pocket that you refuse to part with? I hope it is not something that you have stolen. Thieves are sent to reform school!" Mistress Cummings' piercing eyes cut a hole right through Charley's pocket as if she had sliced it with a knife.

"It ain't stolen!" Charley pulled the comb out his pocket, holding onto it for a second before he placed it in the empty box. Charley exhaled, whistling through his teeth. He felt bone tired. He no longer possessed the strength to fight back. All eyes were glued on the comb. No one spoke. Even Mistress Cummings was silent, and then, shaking her head in disbelief, she looked at Charley and said, "That is a mother-of-pearl hair comb! Where did the likes of you get such a thing?"

"It was my ma's. She wore it in her hair on special days like Christmas and when she took us all to church. She got it from her ma."

He dropped his prize shooter marble and his beloved penknife into the box. Mistress Cummings put a lid on each of the boxes and asked them for their full names. She wrote them down and placed each box in the wooden cabinet and locked it with a skeleton key. "They will be safe, only I and Reverend Matthews have a key. Now, Minnie, come with me; it is off to the nurse with you!"

Charley felt as if there were weights tied to his ankles as he and Clarence climbed the steps to the boys' ward. At the top step, a friendly-looking young man greeted them. "Hello, my name is Thomas. Welcome to the New England Home for Little Wanderers! I was a little wanderer once myself. Reverend Matthews told me to be on the lookout for you. I'm here to help you through the first steps of getting settled. You both look like you've seen a ghost! Don't worry; this is not such a bad place once you get past Mistress Cummings!"

Charley and Clarence glanced at each other and shrugged their shoulders. Charley pinched his nose, crinkling it up like he smelled something putrid. Clarence snickered, "Ya, she sure is a mean old battle axe."

"Come on, follow me, boys. We got some work to do!" He led them down a long hallway passing by many unknown rooms. Charley tried to get a glimpse inside the ones with the doors slightly ajar. But Thomas hurried them along, escorting them into yet another empty room. Charley noticed there was not a stick of furniture in the room, just a metal door on the wall. "Okay guys, take off all your clothes including shoes and throw them down this chute." Thomas lifted the door open as he spoke.

"I ain't gonna get undressed in front of nobody. These here clothes have done me fine and I can go on wearin' 'em jus' fine." Charley crossed his arms over his chest and stuck out his chin in defiance.

Clarence followed his lead. "Me too! I ain't taken no clothes off, no way, no how."

Thomas laughed a deep hearty laugh. "Hey guys, a hot tub is ready for you in the bathing room. I got some nice clean towels sitting there waiting for you. If it will make you feel better, I will step into the next room and hand them back to you so you can cover yourself till you hop into the tub. And by the way, you better get used to it; everyone here takes a bath once a week!"

Thomas did as he promised and handed Charley and Clarence a towel. Then he busied himself getting the pails of water ready for the rinse cycle. The two boys undressed rapidly, wrapping themselves up like mummies in the towels. Charley opened the door to the bathroom, allowing Clarence to go in first. Clarence skidded on the wet tiled floor, landing smack on his behind. Thomas and Charley broke into peals of riotous laughter. Clarence, red faced, threw off the towel and hopped into the tub.

"Yahhhooouuuggh! It's durn boilin' hot!"

Thomas, still chuckling, handed Clarence a bar of soap. "Go to it, old boy, you need it plenty hot. You got years of city grit to wash off your hide."

Charley, with towel wrapped around him, whistled Minnie's tune of, "Tu-ra lu-ra lu-ra, tu-ra lu-ra lie, tu-ra lu-ra lu-ra, hush now don't you cry." He watched Clarence slide the bar of soap down his arm leaving a streak of white behind. He thought about Minnie and how scared she must be.

"Heads up! Here comes the rinse." Thomas picked up a bucket of steaming water and poured it over Clarence's head.

⊷═◉ ◉═⊷

Charley was dressed in his new duds. They felt good. His new tweed jacket fit him perfectly. His boots shined his reflection back up at him when he looked down. He could even wiggle his toes in them. And the best part was that his knickers were not too tight; he could bend his knees without cutting off his circulation. A jaunty new cap that matched his new jacket topped off his outfit. His curls, shaved close to his head, behaved for once, hidden beneath his cap.

"Hey, Clarence, hurry up. Maybe Minnie will be down in the dining room today."

Clarence grumbled, "Hold your horses, Charley. I got trouble gettin' these here dumb boots to tie up right. Besides, Thomas told us Minnie was in isolation 'cause of her havin' lice and a runny nose."

"It's been a week now; they gotta let her out soon. If they don't, I'm gonna go get her out myself!" Charley stomped his foot, enjoying the smacking sound it made on the polished floor. "Here's the bell, come on Clarence, hurry it up or we'll be late. I'm starvin'!"

"Okay, I'm comin'! But if I trip and kill myself on these rotten laces, you're the one to blame." Clarence shuffled out of his dormitory room. The other boys who slept in the room were gone; all that was left were the neatly made beds lined up in rows. Charley had been assigned a room with the older boys. He hadn't made any friends yet and he hadn't planned to. Why should he waste his time? He figured they would get a family soon enough and be out of there.

Charley scanned the dining room. There, sitting up across the room at a table full of girls, was Minnie. "Look! There's Minnie! They cut her hair short like a boys!"

Minnie, seeing her brothers, jumped up from the table and ran to them. "My Charley! My Clarence! I am so happy to see you! I've been in the nurse's room for so long. My cold is all better. The nurse and Mistress Renée took care of me! They had to cut my hair, but I don't mind—it had bugs in it. They put this smelly stuff on it to kill the bugs; it made my eyes cry." Charley looked at his sister as if she was someone he didn't know. Her cheeks were pink and her eyes were clear, not glassy like before, and her nose was clean. She was pretty even with her hair cut short.

Reverend Matthews cleared his throat. He stood tall at the top of the main dining room table. "Please sit down children. It is time to bless our food and say grace."

Minnie stood on tip toes and whispered into Charley's ear, "Come to my table after you eat; I want you to meet Mistress Renée." Then she scurried back to her seat.

Charley and Clarence found two empty seats together at the end of a long table filled with boys. They folded their hands and bowed their heads and waited for Reverend Matthews to finish. Then they ate their breakfast with gusto. Glasses were filled to the brim with fresh milk, and pancakes dripped with sweet maple syrup, crisscrossed with strips of crunchy bacon. The boys ate like they had never seen food before. Charley wanted to lick the sweet syrup off of his plate, but when Clarence had licked the chicken gravy off of his plate the other night, Mistress Cummings had a real tizzy fit. The only thing bad about the Home so far, besides the baths, was the manners. Charley thought that they were all too sticky about silly things like manners.

On their first night, Reverend Matthews had demonstrated to the newcomers how to stack the silverware. "First you place your knife across your plate, like so. Then directly on top of the knife you place your fork, and finally you top the pile off with your spoon." The boys took their knives and followed his lead, carefully balancing knife, fork and then spoon on their plates. "Well done, lads, well done. You will find that when it is your turn to clear the tables, this little ritual will make the job much easier." Charley stacked his silverware now after every meal, but first he made sure to lick them clean.

Mistress Cummings rose from her chair and clapped her hands exactly three times. "Children, please stack your silverware on your plates. You may be dismissed to the playground. The bell for school will ring at 8:10 sharp."

Minnie flew across the dining hall and grabbed onto Charley's jacket, pulling it back and forth, "Come quick, Charley! Before Mistress Renée has to go!" Charley didn't want to meet this Miss Renée, but he allowed Minnie to direct him to her table. He didn't want to hurt his sister's feelings, but he really had had enough of these mistresses!

As they approached the table, a young woman turned her head towards Charley, greeting him with a warm smile. Charley caught himself sucking in his breath. An instantaneous blush illuminated his face like a bright red beacon. "Mistress Renée, this is my brother Charley, the one with the pretty singing! And Clarence, my other brother, he can sing, too." Minnie's face glowed with pride. Charley wanted to die, to disappear into thin air, to dive under the table, to do anything to remove himself from this embarrassing moment. How could Minnie do this to him in front of all these gawking girls? And in front of her!

"*Enchanté!* I am most charmed to meet you, Charley and Clarence." She tucked an escaped curl behind her ear. "Your sweet sister Minnie has told me all about you while she was so sick." Her dark eyes glistened with enthusiasm as she inspected the two boys. "I do hope you will try out for my choir!" Charley blinked. She was the most beautiful woman he had ever seen. She was like a painting in a book he once saw in the Boston Public Library. Her voice was soft and lilting as if she were reciting poetry from a faraway land. Her charm captivated him. He could not speak, his jaw clenched tight, his vocal cords were paralyzed. Feeling like a fool, he nodded his head up and down. "*Merci*, Charley! That is simply wonderful, I am so happy. We have try-outs today before lunch in the choir room. I look forward to hearing your exquisite voice! And you too, Clarence and Minnie, *mon amie!* You must all try out for my choir."

◆══○ CHAPTER 5 ○══◆

The Concert

Charley stood frozen in the doorway of the choir hall. He watched as Mistress Renée handed out sheets of music and fussed over where each child should stand. "The little ones must come to the front. I want to see each one of your beautiful faces. How can I hear you if you are hiding behind someone taller than yourself! Minnie, *mon amie*, you come over here." She took Minnie's hand and led

her to the front spot in the center. "I am so happy that you are here to try out for my traveling choir. And Clarence, you must come over here, in the second row, there, now I can see you. I do hope your brother is coming."

"There's Charley. Over there by the door." Clarence pointed his finger in Charley's direction. Minnie ran to him. "Come, Charley! You must sing!" Mistress Renée turned to welcome him. Every set of eyes in the choir stared at him, burning holes in his new clothes. His plan had been to slip into the music room unnoticed. He wanted to listen for a while before he committed himself to joining any choir. He wasn't really sure he wanted to do this singing thing at all, even if Minnie and the choir lady happened to trick him into stupidly nodding yes.

"Charley, *mon ami!* I am so happy to see that you came! Please do not be shy. Come and join us; we do not bite!" Mistress Renée's dark brown eyes twinkled with encouragement. "Let's see, how about if you stand just behind Clarence. Here is your sheet music. Everyone ready? First, we will do our warm ups." She walked a few steps towards an upright piano. "As I play the notes on the piano I want you to sing out with all your chest power. Stand up straight, pull in your stomachs, shoulders back and sing! I don't want to hear any squeaks!"

Charley couldn't stop looking at her. He still felt foolish. He shouldn't have come. He didn't know what she meant about warm ups or singing notes or chest power. Couldn't they just sing? How hard could that be? He wished he were somewhere else, hanging around down by the wharf or squeezing through a window. He knew how to do that!

Mistress Renée plucked the piano key and the group sang out, "La." She hit a higher note and the choir answered her with a resounding, "LA!" And then another and another, Charley caught on quick. It wasn't hard. All he had to do was mimic the sound she played on the piano. That was easy! He could hear a song or melody just once and repeat it with perfect pitch, just like his dad.

"Excellent, you are sounding *magnifique* today! Now let's do our scales." She played a long string of notes going from low to high and back down again. The choir answered her each time she played. "*Extraordinaire!* You are my little nightingales! Now that we are warmed up who would like to go first? Charley, you are the oldest of our tryouts today. How would you like to sing first? Let's try the first song on the top of page two, entitled 'It Is All for the Best.' I will start you off with the key of C." She nodded her head at Charley as she plunked down a piano key.

"La!" came out of Charley's mouth in perfect imitation of the note she played. The boy next to him snickered. He could feel his cheeks burning. Did he do something dumb?

"Excellent, Charley! Now just read the notes and sing the first verse for me in the key of C."

He wanted to die, right there, just curl up and die. This was too painful to imagine. He looked down at the paper and saw flags with lines and circles dancing up and down the page. None of it made the least bit of sense. How could he sing the song if he didn't know the melody? Was she trying to make him look stupid? She had seemed so nice, but now he wanted to be as far away from her as he could get!

Charley's temper boiled hot inside him, he would not be made a fool of. He pushed Clarence aside and walked up to the teacher. He handed her his sheets of music and said, "I don't know this song. I can't sing it."

Her face transformed from a look of shock to one of utter and complete understanding. "Oh, Charley! *Excusez-moi!* I am so terribly sorry. Please forgive me. I will have the choir sing the song and then you will know it, am I right?"

"Yes, ma'am, if I hear it, I can sing it." Charley watched as the choir, directed by Mistress Renée's capable hands, burst into song. He followed along with the words and watched how the flags floated up and down with the melody as they sang. By the second verse he started to sing along with the choir. At first he sang in a whisper mouthing the words, then as the song built its tempo so did he. He could see the song in his mind and feel it in his heart. He couldn't stop himself. His voice rang out clear and strong with perfect pitch. The boy next to him stopped singing and listened in awed silence. Several more stopped and stared at Charley with their mouths half open. Soon Charley was the only one singing, his voice flowing from light and lilting to deep and resonant as he crescendoed to a sudden stop at the end of the last verse.

Mistress Renée, her head perfectly erect above her starched high-necked blouse and large puffy sleeves, stood motionless and speechless. Her hands, clasped together in front of her slender waist, did not move. She stared at

Charley, as if she were somehow trying to comprehend what she had just heard. Then she threw her hands up into the air and cried out joyfully, "Welcome to my traveling choir, Charley! I think I will place you exactly in the middle of the choir right between the sopranos and altos, with my few tenors behind you. Now Clarence and Minnie, it is your turn!"

→→◎ ◎←←

"Charley, hurry! We'll be late for our first concert! Eat fast or take it with you!" Minnie jumped up and down. The soles of her new high-top shoes made a tap dancing sound on the marble floor. Minnie radiated happiness. Charley had been surprised how pretty she looked all cleaned up and dressed in a proper dress that fit her. Minnie laughed and shook a finger at Charley. "Mistress Renée will not be pleased with you! She will say you can't sing your solo today!"

Charley grabbed three rolls of sweet bread and stuffed them inside his coat. "I'm comin'! You're just a nervous Nellie 'bout your first time singin' in front of people!"

"I am so excited, Charley; we get to stand way up front of the church and sing to all those people. Do you think they will be pleased with us?"

"You bet they will! We might even be lucky enough to find ourselves a home today!" Charley started down the steps of the dining room with Minnie following on his heels.

"Really, Charley? Really do you think so?"

"When people go to church they feel all godly and good inside. That's why Mistress Renée brings us to sing to them, to make 'em want to take us home." Charley swung the giant mahogany door open, and he and Minnie raced down the steps to the street below.

"Minnie, Charley, come quickly, the trolley is here to take us to King's Chapel." Mistress Renée waved her gloved hand in the air as the trolley screeched to a halt. She counted each head as they climbed the two steps into the trolley car. Thirty-two heads. She would count them many times before this Sunday was over. She showed the conductor her pass and found herself a seat as the trolley lurched forward. The trolley ride was a living adventure. They were the lucky ones! The trips to the churches and community halls were exciting; just sitting in a seat and riding legally inside a trolley was exhilarating.

At the Park Street stop, Mistress Renée ushered them out the door onto the crowded city street. She touched the top of thirty-two heads. "Follow close behind me, I do not want to lose any of you!" She led her troupe the two blocks down Tremont Street to the entrance of King's Chapel. The children filed into the back of the church silently to await their introduction at the end of the service. A poster was hanging in the entryway. Charley read the large fancy letters:

The Children's Choir from the New England Home For Little Wanderers will sing following Sunday service on the fourteenth of December in the year of Our Lord 1910. Please remain seated throughout the entire concert. *Good Christian Families are needed to provide these children with a loving home. Please direct all inquires to the Choir Mistress immediately after the concert.*

Charley wondered if today would be the day they found a family. The service droned on and on and the sermon took forever. Charley felt queasy in his stomach. Maybe he shouldn't have eaten so many sweet breads. His hands felt cold and clammy. He rubbed them together and blew on them to warm them up. Was he getting stage fright? There sure were a lot of people stuffed into this church. It was a grand church, he thought, it must have been around a long time.

Finally the minister, clearing his throat, addressed the congregation. "This morning we are honored to welcome the very well known children's choir from the New England Home for Little Wanderers. Choir Mistress, please accompany your children to the front of the church." Mistress Renée, her head held high in a woven bonnet tied with a bright yellow ribbon, led her choir down the long carpeted aisle. Charley could hear hushed whispers as they walked past the ends of the pews. Mistress Renée ordered them to fall into their assigned formation. Then she turned to greet the congregation.

"*Bonjour!* Good morning! We are very proud indeed to be singing at King's Chapel! The children have worked long and hard to present you with an inspirational concert. The songs they will sing for you today are listed in your bulletins. We will conclude the concert with the 'Hallelujah Chorus.' Immediately following the concert I will be available to speak with any families that would like to give one of these fine children a home. Please remember that some children are born into loving families while others, just as deserving, have not been given a fair chance in life. All they need is your love and kindness. Thank you for your attention. And now the choir will begin with our very own song, 'It Is All for the Best!'"

Following Mistress Renée's expert direction, the children sang better than they had ever sung before. The great stone church was still except for the voices that rose higher and higher, reaching the towering heights of the chapel spires themselves. Mouths dropped open and hankies were tugged out of purses as the children entranced the congregation with their angelic voices. After three verses, Charley stepped forward and sang the fourth verse solo. He had never sung in a chapel or cathedral before. His voice embraced the entire church; the pews, the walls, the ceiling and the people. The congregation listened with awed admiration as he held the last note until Mistress Renée released him with a wave of her hand. One man clapped his hands and then another. Soon the whole church rang out with a deafening applause. Charley caught his breath and bowed. Flushed and happy, he stepped back into position.

The concert ended with everyone singing along with the "Hallelujah Chorus." Thunderous applause filled the church.

The kids in the choir stood rigid, waiting and watching

as a number of families came forward to speak to Mistress
Renée. A man and a woman, dressed in fine clothes, were
the first to approach. The lady was tall and stylish in a
tailored suit with a lace flower pinned to the lapel of her
jacket. The man cut a handsome profile in a dark striped
suit, his bowler hat tucked under his arm. Charley thought
they must be millionaires. One of the boys had told him
on the trolley ride that this was a fancy pants church!

The lady was smiling at Minnie. Charley's heart
stopped in his chest. He hit Clarence with his elbow. "Hey!
Watcha hittin' me for?" Clarence shoved Charley back.

"Look at that lady! She's lookin' at Minnie." Charley
sucked his breath in, swallowing his spit, which made him
cough.

"Hey, you're right, Charley; they're talkin' to her. She's
laughin' and talkin' back. What do you think it means,
Charley?" Clarence screwed his face up in confusion.
Charley pushed past the kids in front of him, he had to
know what was being said.

"Oh! That is so very kind of you! Minnie is a wonderful little girl. I have some paperwork that you must sign
and a worker from the Home will come out to visit Minnie
and make sure she settles in well." Mistress Renée leaned
down to hug Minnie and whispered something in her ear.
Minnie nodded her head and clapped her hands in delight.
Charley and Clarence came forward, almost falling on top
of Minnie.

"Oh, Charley! Clarence! I am going to visit Mr. and
Mrs. Taylor for a whole week. They live in a big house on

a hill right here in Boston and they have two little dogs named Peter Pan and Wendy Darling. They said I can walk them in the Boston Public Gardens with all the pretty flowers. Mrs. Taylor said that there are boats there that look like swans, and we can go for a ride on them." Minnie's face was radiant! She threw her arms around her two brothers. "I will come back soon! I'll miss you both terribly!" Then she spun around on her heels. The lady took Minnie's hand, and joined by the gentleman, they walked down the aisle as a threesome. Charley and Clarence, with their mouths open, stood there dumbfounded. The two brothers watched as three more children left to go home with new families that day.

Mistress Renée counted the heads as they boarded the trolley. Charley was the last one. He held back hoping to get a glimpse of Minnie, but she had disappeared from sight. She was gone. Charley felt like someone had kicked him in the stomach. How could this be happening? The plan was for the three of them to stay together! How could Minnie walk away with people she never even met? Who were they anyways? How dare they take his sister and leave him and Clarence behind? He felt helpless and abandoned. He kicked his toe hard against the curbstone, scraping the tip of his new boot. He pulled his cap down as far as it would go; he didn't want the others to see how miserable and cheated he felt.

"Hurry, Charley! You must get on the trolley." His feet felt like lead as he forced himself to take the two steps into the trolley. Mistress Renée tapped his head and counted, "Twenty-eight."

⊶⇒ CHAPTER 6 ⇐⊷

A Penny Pickle

Charley's fist hit the huge mahogany door. He pulled his clenched hand backwards aiming for another hard blow. The door swung open revealing the startled face of Reverend Matthews. "Charley, is anything wrong? Is there an emergency?"

"I need to talk to you, sir. It's important, sir."

"Come in, come in and sit down. Now, Charley, what can I do for you?"

"Sir, my sister, Minnie, went home with a man and a woman from the church concert. Is she going to stay there and live with them? Are they going to be her family? Minnie said she was staying for only a week. A week is over, sir, and soon it will be Christmas. Clarence and I gotta know, because, you see, sir, we were supposed to stay together." Charley's eyes, red around the rims, begged for an answer. He had tried to talk to Mistress Renée, but she suggested he speak to Reverend Matthews himself.

"My boy, I do understand your concern. As a matter of fact I was just reviewing the case and it seems the social worker has already been to visit Minnie at her placement with the Taylors. It turns out, Charley, she is very happy there. The Taylors are fine Christian people. She will be given all the things in life that she deserves. You would want the best for your sister, wouldn't you? It is not that she is far away. Minnie is living right here in Boston, so you and Clarence will be able to visit her on Christmas day."

Charley's hand slammed down on Reverend Matthews's desk, scattering papers with its impact. Charley felt burning anger churning in his stomach and encircling his brain like a tight band. He was furious that he had been tricked. "Are you saying that Minnie has found a good Christian family and Clarence and I don't fit in? Sir, you said, the day we came here, you said to George, that you would do everything to keep us together! You let Minnie go to a family by herself, and next it will be Clarence! And I, I will be here by myself! Families don't want older boys. I know, I ain't dumb, the guys told me. Look at Howard. He's been here forever. I don't think it's fair; I don't think it's right. I don't think you should be splittin' families up!"

"Now, Charley, calm yourself. Minnie is not being adopted, since your father is still alive that cannot happen. Her placement is a temporary placement. So far, she is happy. Please be patient and try to understand that things don't always work out the way we think they should. Our job is to find the best home for each child. When your turn comes, hopefully, we can keep you and Clarence together. We do prefer that siblings stay together whenever they can. I will need you to be brave about your sister's placement and wish the best for her."

Charley could tell it was hopeless to talk the Reverend

out of Minnie's placement, but he had to make his final point about him and Clarence. "All right, sir, but you have to promise to keep Clarence and me together!"

Reverend Matthews tugged on his beard and, smiling his fatherly smile, he said, "I promise I will do my best for you and your brother. Now, Charley, I have a job for you. One that I think you will like. Some very important people are coming this afternoon to view the Home. How would you like to be their tour guide? All you have to do is show them around and at the end bring them to the choir room. There Mistress Renée will be waiting with the choir to perform a holiday concert for our guests. Do you think you could help me out with this? If you do well, I will pay you a penny."

Charley's head was spinning. Reverend Matthews was trying to trick him. He had no intentions of forgetting about Minnie or her placement. Still, Charley thought the offer sounded worth considering. He'd heard the boys say that the lucky ones that got picked to give tours to the fancy people were in good with the reverend. And he did pay them. Everyday chores like clearing tables and taking the sheets down to the laundry were boring. But giving tours to rich city people from Boston, now that was a big deal.

"Can I do what I want with the penny, or does it go into my box?"

"The penny is yours, Charley. I promise no one will take it from you."

"Can I go down the street and buy me one of those big pickles at Smitty's shop?" Charley had been eyeing that pickle barrel and his mouth was watering for a big juicy one right now.

Reverend Matthews laughed. "Yes, Charley! You may buy yourself a penny pickle."

"It's a deal!"

CHAPTER 7

A Proper Gentleman

Charley pulled the covers over his head. His ears rung and his head throbbed with pain. He stifled a nearly escaped sob. He must not cry. The boys would hear him. The events of the day haunted him. He tried over and over to make some sense of them. They rattled around in his brain like Mexican jumping beans. Was he going crazy? Should he climb out the window? He could go back out on the streets. He would find George.

Christmas had been a disaster. The visit with Minnie was way too short. The Taylors dropped her off for one stinkin' hour. And George arrived late. He hardly got to see her before the social worker returned to take Minnie back to the Taylors' home. She cried and begged to stay longer, and then George got mad and yelled some cuss words at the social worker. That didn't do any good, the lady got all snippety and took Minnie by the hand and led her away.

Now Clarence was gone too, just like Minnie. Gone to a stupid farm! Clarence didn't know the first thing about being a farmer. All the reasons given to Charley for staying at the Home were gone. Why should he stay? How could he trust Mistress Renée ever again? Not after today, never ever again, not after today!

He made up his mind, he would go out on his own, George or no George. He lay still, listening to the deep breathing of sleeping boys. Charley, fully dressed, slipped out of bed. He grabbed his boots and rounded the corner of the dormitory doorway entering the long dark hall. A lamp shone outside the younger boys' dorm, where Clarence had slept. He had to get past that and down the stairs. Mistress Cummings' room was up on the third floor. She made the rounds on the hour and Charley had heard her footsteps go by awhile ago. He held his breath as he scurried past the lit doorway. He reached the stairs and took them two at a time. He checked the first floor offices. All the doors were locked tight so there was no access to a window. His only hope was to force open one of the casement windows in the basement. He had often seen the housekeeper open them during the day to air out the cellar, but she closed them at night to keep the animals out. Charley bounded down the final flight of stairs, finding himself in a dark and musty-smelling cellar. PU! He scrunched his nose. It smelled like a dead cat or worse!

His eyes had to adjust to the darkness of the basement but soon he spotted a battered chair. He pushed it underneath a window. Half the seat had rotted away. He balanced with his feet straddling the hole in the chair. Stretching on his tiptoes, his fingers investigated the window casement searching for the latch. His fingertips just grazed the bottom tip of it. Darn! A few more inches would do it. If Big Dan were here, Charley thought, he would have me through in a second. He got down off the chair and looked around for something to raise himself up. Propped against the wall was a nice thick board; it was longer than he wanted, but he thought it should work. He positioned the board on the chair and placed his right foot on it. He grabbed the back of the chair to steady himself as he hoisted himself up. Bam! The board flew upwards, hitting him smack on the side of his head. Charley and the chair toppled sideways. He hit the floor full force, the board landing on top of him. He lay there stunned. His rib cage felt as if he had been whacked with an axe. He pushed the board off of himself and tried to sit up. A sharp pain shot through him. He heard footsteps running down the stairs. A sudden light lit up the stairway. "Oh no, not Mistress Cummings!" Charley groaned out loud.

"Charley, *mon ami*! Whatever are you doing down here? I heard this terrible bang. Have you hurt yourself? Let me help you." Charley couldn't believe it. There, bending over him, was Mistress Renée!

"I don't understand Charley! What were you trying to do? Go out through the window? Why would you want to do such a thing? What would I do without you? My soloist? I need you in my choir, Charley! Oh, you would not run away, would you?"

Charley tried to raise himself up. Mistress Renée helped to prop him into a sitting position. Charley closed his eyes and leaned against the wall. He tried to gather himself together. The scene after the concert still fresh, stung sharp, like a slap across his face. She betrayed him! A traitor! He couldn't stand it any longer. Accusations exploded out of him, "Why? Why did you send the gentleman away? I saw him speak to you. He pointed at me. He was a proper gentleman. You sent him away! Why?"

"Oh, *mon ami*, you do not understand these things. It is not so very simple as you think. I could not allow that man to take you away. I would never let you go with just anyone." Pulling a hanky from her sleeve, she offered it to him. Charley pulled away from her.

"You let Minnie go with the Taylors and you didn't know them. You let Clarence go to a farm that you've never ever seen. Why? Why would you ruin my chance, my only chance?"

"I am explaining to you, Charley. Please, please try to understand. I could never let you go with that man; he was not good enough for you."

"How can you say he wasn't good enough? What is good enough? I'm not good enough!" Hot tears escaped down his cheeks. Angry with himself for crying, he rubbed his sleeve across his face, smearing the tears. His chest heaved; it hurt dull and deep inside.

Mistress Renée shook her head in disagreement. "No, Charley, I would not let you go with him. I had good reason. He smelled of whiskey! Yes, he was dressed up in all his fine clothes showing off that he had lots of money. But a man that comes to church smelling of alcohol is not good enough for you! I wish, I wish, I only wish . . . well, never mind. Let me see if we can get you back upstairs to bed." Charley allowed her to lift his arm over her shoulders, and then gently pull him to his feet. Slow and steady they traveled the short distance to the stairway. Step by step they climbed the two flights of stairs.

As they ended their journey to his room, Charley stiffened, pulling away from her. He didn't want to be seen leaning on Mistress Renée. "I can walk by myself." Then he said, "My pa smelled like whiskey too, and sure enough, he left us."

⟶ CHAPTER 8 ⟵

The Girl with Braids

Charley stared out the window of the train. He wanted to see the state of Maine. He had never been out of Boston before. The train steamed along through small towns with church steeples, farms with rolling fields and acres and acres of forest. "Jeepers, this is summer in the country," Charley thought. "I ain't ever seen so much green. Must be why they call this place we're going to Greene, Maine."

Mistress Renée passed out sandwiches wrapped in white waxy paper from her wicker basket. She handed one to Charley and one to Tim who was sitting next to him. "For lunch today we have the very best German baloney, with mustard, on fresh homemade bread, and a sugar cookie for dessert. *Bon appétit!*"

Charley's stomach growled like a bear. He was always hungry. He often got teased about how much he could pack away at one sitting. Mistress Renée said he wore it all away when he sang. Reverend Matthews told him he must have a hollow leg. Mistress Cummings just scowled at him. Charley wished all the food he ate would grow him a couple more inches. Many of the younger boys were taller than he. He tried not to let it bother him, but it did.

"Hey Charley, wadja think about we go for another

sandwich? I seen she brings extras!" Tim was a big kid and dumber than anything. Charley figured Tim would need at least three sandwiches to keep him happy.

"Eat what you got before you go beggin' for more," Charley snapped back at him.

Tim chomped down on his sandwich, severing it in half. He chewed with his mouth open making smacking noises. He swallowed in one gulp, then belched. "I sure am hopin' I get a durn decent family. The last one didn't work out so good; that's why I had ta come back. That old man was a mean bugger, all he wanted outta me was to work me ta death, morning till night, and then the lady she give us some scraps ta eat, couldn't even tell what they was. Looked the same as what she gave the dogs." Tim shoved the other half of the sandwich in his mouth. He wiped the stain of mustard around his mouth with the edge of his sleeve.

"Hey Charley, did you see what happened at the station? The durned skirt fell right off Betty Lou and landed smack on the platform?" Tim chuckled with pleasure at the poor girl's plight.

"Ya I did, Mistress Renée saved her, she got her back in her skirt and sewed it up fast, just the minute the train came roarin' in!"

Secretly Charley wondered why Mistress Renée had never married. She would make someone a good mother. She sure was pretty and smart. And she made great sandwiches too!

Charley, lost in his thoughts, tried to ignore Tim's yakin' away at him. "Ya know Charley, we is goin' to some big time farmin' country. These Maine people are gonna be lookin' for workhorses. You know how they puts up them posters before we come? It's kinda embarrassing 'cause they ain't lookin' for no sons or daughter; theys lookin' for slaves! They'll work ya till there ain't nothin' left, then they sell your hide to the glue factory like an old horse!"

"Cut it out! You're just latherin' yourself up. Stop worryin', you'll find a family. You just had bad luck with the first one, that's all." Charley wanted him to shut up. He wished he hadn't sat next to him. He didn't want to be mean; the kid had had a bad time of it. But Charley needed to hang on to his hopes of finding himself a family. He had just celebrated his birthday last month. The cook made him a cake. It had twelve candles on it, and he blew every one of them out. He had wished for a family of his own. He didn't want to be like Howard, thirteen years old and still in an orphanage. Tim rankled him because deep down he knew Tim was right about one thing. They would want tall strong boys with muscles to work on the farms. That meant he didn't have a ghost of a chance, not here, not in farm country, not in Greene, Maine.

Mistress Renée passed by, slipping each boy another sandwich and two sugar cookies.

⟢⟤

Charley spotted her right away. From his riser in the front of the church, he had a perfect view of the parishioners sitting in their pews. She was fidgeting in her seat. Her mother, soft and pretty and round, with a baby perched on

her lap, leaned over to speak to her. The girl grinned a wide grin, her brown eyes sparkling with delight. She wore a straw bonnet tied under her chin with a blue satin bow. Her sandy brown hair, tightly braided, cascaded down the front of her starched pinafore. On the other side of the mother sat a younger girl contentedly paging through a prayer book. Next to her sat the father, upright and stern, with a bushy black beard. And next to him sat his son; silent, tall and square jawed.

The choir sang their usual lineup of songs: "It's All for the Best," "Count Your Blessings" and "I Know My Heavenly Father Knows." Lastly, Mistress Renée conducted the "Hallelujah Chorus," inviting everyone to join in. The congregation, greatly moved by the children's voices, accepted the invitation. Charley watched the girl with the braids sing. She sang as if she were the only one in the church. He couldn't single out her voice but he had a hunch that she was terribly off key. Watching her made him feel good inside. She reminded him of Minnie, just a little bit.

After the last hallelujah, the congregation burst into applause. Mistress Renée, beaming with pride, motioned for Charley to come forward. He had sung his very best solo ever! The applause heightened as he bent into a sweeping bow. The choir bowed once more and then the concert was officially over. The moment Charley dreaded. The congregation started to disperse into the aisles, but several families lagged behind in their pews. One of these that stayed was the family with the girl. The mother and father were speaking to each other over the children's heads. The girl with the braids was jumping up and down in her seat and pointing towards the choir. Charley's heart was pounding right out of his chest. His knees felt as if they were made of rubber. The father stood up and walked to the front of the church. Mistress Renée was speaking with a man and woman surrounded by a gaggle of children. He waited patiently for her to finish. The man and woman had chosen Howard. Charley watched as the boy awkwardly joined the group. Howard stood a full head above the children. Charley's eyes followed them as they walked out of the church together. He wondered if Howard would be happy.

Charley's mouth was dry. His tongue was glued to the roof of his mouth. Tim was punching him in the back. He wanted to turn around and knock his block off. This was important! Were they going to pick him? Charley was afraid to listen but at the same time he strained to hear. He desperately wanted to be chosen this time. He didn't want to be alone anymore, traveling from place to place singing and hoping and never being the one that was picked. He yearned to have a home, a mother and a father and some kids to grow up with.

The father didn't look in Charley's direction, but spoke directly to Mistress Renée, holding his hat in his hands. She acted perplexed as she pointed past Charley towards Tim. Was he asking about Tim? Charley's hopes shattered to bits like a glass window when a rock goes through it. He knew he had not one smattering of a chance. The farmer would never pick him. Count them! Go ahead! Count them, he told himself. The man has one son and two daughters and a baby. Of course he would pick the biggest and the strongest boy to help on the farm. Tim was right. They would work him to death. Maybe it was better that he stayed with the choir and Mistress Renée. The man spoke in such a low voice that Charley couldn't make out what he was saying. Then the father turned from Mistress Renée and walked back to the pew where his family was waiting. The mother put the baby in the braided girl's lap and scurried to the end of the pew seeming intensely anxious to hear what her husband had to say. He spoke with his head bent so only she could hear. She responded by shaking her head back and forth in a decisive "No!" She spoke fast, her hands going up and down. The children of the family sat silently while their parents debated. The father's face, as if carved out of stone, never changed expression. When the mother was finished, she smiled at the father and gently stroked the arm of his coat.

The father, with long strides, walked back up the aisle to Mistress Renée. His hat still in his hands he stood before her and said, "My wife would like the boy who sings."

CHAPTER 9

The Worthingtons

"May I ask your name, sir?" inquired Mistress Renée, rising to her full height of five feet two inches.

"Yes, ma'am, the name is Worthington, Edwin Worthington. My wife's name is Mary."

"Well, Mr. Worthington, I understand that your wife wants a boy that sings; that is fine because all of our boys sing! As I have already pointed out, Timothy would be an excellent choice for you. Now there is just a simple form to fill out and then a social worker will come at a future date to approve the placement."

"Ma'am, my wife would like the boy that sings alone."

Charley had pushed his way forward and was standing right behind Mistress Renée's long, flowing skirt. Charley's heart leapt. Did he say, "The boy that sings alone?" Does that mean me? Charley's head was spinning. They want me?

"Mr. Worthington, do you intend to use this boy as free labor on your farm?" she asked curtly.

"Well, ma'am, we would be expecting him to help with farm chores like every member of our family. We are good Christian people, and we would be willing to give this boy a wholesome home. What is the lad's name?"

"Charley. My name is Charles Kimball Ryan." He scooted out from behind Mistress Renée and positioned himself in front of her. This was his chance! He had to fight for it. "I am glad to meet you, sir, um, Mr. Worthington." He held out his hand, but it was shaking so badly he put it back in his jacket pocket.

"Young man, if are you in agreement to come and live in our home, then we would be willing for you to come along home with us."

"Yes, sir. I mean, um, I'm in agreement." Charley's head was reeling. Was this really happening? Was he to go home with this family? The girl with braids had wiggled her way out of the pew and now ran up the aisle to her father's side. She shone like a bright new penny. The younger sister shyly snuggled in next to her. The mother joined the circle, bouncing the baby up and down in her arms. The son sat silent and alone back in the pew.

"Mr. Worthington, I want you all to understand that this would only be a trial placement. In time, a social worker will pay a call to your farm. If Charley's needs are not being met or he is unhappy, he will return to the Home. We, at the New England Home for Little Wanderers, do not give our children away to be farm laborers. And we insist that the child attends school until they are fourteen years of age." Mistress Renée's voice sounded far away and distant to Charley. He was anxious to go, he didn't want her to ruin his only chance, and yet now that it was all happening so fast he felt a sudden sadness creeping over him. He would miss her. He would miss singing for her. She had been as gentle and kind as he could imagine any real mother would be.

"Don't worry 'bout me, Mistress Renée. I will be fine."
Charley spoke bravely. Then he whispered in her ear. "I
need my box; can you bring it to me?"

"Oh, Charley, I may not soon have the opportunity to
come all this way again. My job is to travel with the choir.
But you must not worry, *mon ami*. I will personally make
sure your box is sent to you. Now we must sadly say *au
revoir*, goodbye my Charley." She leaned towards him to kiss
the top of his head. Charley threw his arms around her.
Tears welled up in his eyes. How could he be so happy and
so miserable at the same moment? He had to force himself
to hold back his feelings; he couldn't let them show; he
couldn't let them see him cry. He pulled himself away, but
part of him stayed with her. He straightened his jacket and
with a shaky voice said, "Please make sure George knows
where I am."

"Yes, Charley, I will let George know." Then she turned
with a swish of her long skirt. She busied herself methodi-
cally tapping the heads of her choir and counting, thirty
less two equals twenty-eight.

⊷⊜ ⊜⊶

Long shadows stretched across the dirt road as the horses
and wagon rambled along in the late afternoon. Mr.
Worthington and his son sat up front. He directed the
horses with a clicking sound he made with the side of his
mouth and a tug of the reins. Other than that, Mr.
Worthington did not utter one word the whole length of
the trip and neither did his son. Mrs. Worthington was

busy quieting the baby that was beginning to fuss. The
girls were the only ones who seemed interested in Charley.
They sat flanking him on either side in the back seat of the
wagon. The younger one looked up at Charley with big
starry eyes. The one with the braids seemed to Charley
like a ticking clock whose alarm was about to go off. She
was the first to break the ice.

"Hi, my name is Laura and I am nine years old." As she
spoke, her one hand untied the ribbon under her chin
while the other whipped the bonnet off her head and with
precision stuck it promptly beneath the seat. "I have my
own rifle and I can shoot me a rabbit faster 'n you kin say
freeze a monkey! You ever shot yourself a critter?" Her eyes
danced with merriment. She threw her head back, crinkled her freckled nose, opened her mouth wide and let out
a wildly contagious belly laugh. Charley knew right then
and there that he had met his match.

"Nope, don't believe I have ever shot a critter with a rifle. But I sure enough caught me some rats by the tail down by the wharf. Big mean ones!" Charley raised his arm upward with his fist clenched. "I was holdin' one big black one by his long pink rat tail when he swung himself around and durn tried to bite me. His teeth were sharp as razors. They cut a hole right through my jacket pocket. I swung him high in the air and he landed splat, back in the water where he'd come from!" Laura and her sister listened entranced.

"Do you got the jacket, the one with the hole in it from the rat?" Laura asked with awe. "Could ya show it to us?"

"Naw, that was my old jacket, they burned all our clothes at the Home."

Laura's eyes just about popped out of her head. "Why'd they burn your clothes?"

"'Cause of bugs and sickness could have been in them. It was okay. They gave us new ones. See my tweed jacket and cap, the seamstress made it just for me."

"Oh! They are swell, Charley! You look mighty fine in 'em. Shoot! You look like a right fine gentleman from the city!" Laura looked down, patting the skirt of her dress. "My Granny Rozella, she makes all our clothes. You'll meet her when we get home; she never goes anywhere; she just stays home and sews."

The horses slowed as they trotted between avenues of giant elm trees. Charley strained forward to see what lay ahead. Mr. Worthington called, "Whoa there, Maud! Whoa there, Chubb!" The son jumped off the wagon and swung open a large wooden gate. Charley, following Laura, climbed out of the back of the wagon. He stood glued to the ground, studying the scene before him. It was like a painting from a book, a big yellow house with shiny white shutters surrounded by a lush green lawn and gardens, encircled by a perfect picket fence. Inside the gardens, massive clumps of flowers and orderly lines of vegetables marched up to the tops of wooden poles like Indian teepees. High-backed rocking chairs rested on a wrap-around porch to welcome a person to sit down and stay awhile.

Next to the house there was a well-worn path that led to a huge, red wooden structure with a small room perched on the top with windows on each side. Charley thought that if you climbed to the top and looked out the windows you would be able to see for miles and miles. The farm itself sat high on the crest of a hill overlooking distant hills and valleys; they stretched so far into the horizon the farthest hills were no more than a soft blue haze. The son unhitched the horses from the wagon and, holding onto their reins, walked beside them down the path. Around a big barn-shaped building were some fenced-in sections and beyond those, as far as Charley could see, there were fields upon fields of waving grass.

Mrs. Worthington climbed down from the wagon and handed the baby to Laura. Her face was warm with kindness. "Welcome to our home, Charley. Let me take you inside and show you around. Harlan will care for the horses, and then he and Mr. Worthington will milk the cows before it gets too late and the ladies start to complain. After cows are milked, we have our supper." She bustled up to the door and swung it open allowing Charley to enter first.

Charley whipped his cap off and took a step into the house. A window was open, allowing the last remnants of sun to filter into the room. A sudden breeze made the curtains billow inward. Then he saw her, sitting upright in a chair with a spindle leg table in front of her. A sewing machine sat perched on top of it. Her foot, never missing a beat, pumped up and down on a trestle pedal that lay just above the floorboards. Her knobby hands moved at a

steady pace guiding a piece of fabric into the direct line of a needle that was whirring so fast it was no more than a blur. Charley froze in his tracks. He had never seen anyone as severe looking as this old lady. She had a square jaw that stuck out hard and sharp. Her broad nose spread across her face into her cheekbones. Three white spit curls of hair were plastered down flat on her forehead. The rest of her hair was hidden behind a white starched cap trimmed with a short ripple of lace. Deeply set, beady eyes darted back and forth as she sewed, dissecting him. Charley shuddered. He immediately had an intense dislike for this woman, and he was sure that she felt the same towards him.

⊷⥤ CHAPTER 10 ⥢⊷

A Prize Shooter

"Come on, Charley! Get up, we gotta get our chores done." Laura took a hold of Charley's covers and gave them a good yank.

"Hey! What time is it anyways?" Charley opened one eye. "It's still dark!" He burrowed further down under his blanket.

"No you don't! You gotta git up! Didn't ya hear the rooster crowin'? We ain't getting' nothin' to eat till them chores is done! Five o'clock is wake up time. You're lucky it's me. Harlan woulda' picked up the whole mattress and rolled ya out on the floor."

Charley poked one reluctant foot out from the covers then pulled it back instantly. "Just give me five more winks."

"Hurry up! Get your chore clothes on. Meet ya at the chicken coop." In the wink of an eye Laura exited Charley's room and as she did so, she bumped smack into her granny.

Granny Rozella hissed at her, "Laura Ann Worthington! Whatever were you doing in that boarder's room?" Charley turned a sleepy ear toward the half-open door to listen while he pulled on his flannel shirt and overalls. His room was small but cozy. The heat of the kitchen stove warmed him through the wall and the door that his room shared with the kitchen. The rest of the family slept on the second floor. He chuckled to himself thinking about Laura sneaking in to wake him. She must have saved him from a nasty awakening by Granny Rozella. He shook his head. His first hunch had been right—that woman, for some reason, had taken an extreme dislike to him. Charley, mostly dressed, peeked out the crack of the door. He could see Laura twisting the knotted suspender that held up her worn blue overalls. She refused to look at her granny. It seemed to Charley that she was biding her time before she answered.

"I was just waking Charley up."

"Girls don't go sneaking around waking boys up from their beds." Granny Rozella tugged on the whiskery hairs that stuck out from her chin. "You just worry about helpin' your hard-working mother in the kitchen. No need to be coddling this waif from the streets. Your brother, Harlan, will be makin' sure he does his share of the chores! He'll sure enough get up out of that bed and get them done if he wants to eat."

Charley, still buttoning his shirt, stepped out of his room. "Top of the morning to you, Granny Rozella. How are you this fine summer morning?"

"Never you mind how I am! Just get those chores done. Harlan has been out in the barn tending the animals since a full half hour ago." She gave her chin hairs a final tug then waddled away muttering, "Boarders! Irish scum in the house!"

"Don't pay no attention to Granny; she doesn't have all her marbles! Ya know what I mean?" Laura twirled her right index finger in the air and then thumped her temple with it.

Charley grinned. "Sure I know what ya mean; I've met lots of crazy people in the city. One guy used ta put a bucket upside down and stand on his head for hours. Every time I passed him by he was upside down, the blood all running into his face makin' him look real scary! He had his hat out in front of him with a sign that said 'pennies for the poor equals a higher place in heaven!'"

"Really Charley! I wish I could go to Boston sometime and see some crazy people."

"Maybe someday we can take the train, but I warn ya it's a heck of a long ride."

Charley and Laura let the door slam behind them as they ventured toward the chicken coop.

Harlan sauntered out from the barn and said, "I'll be showin' mornin' chores to ya. Laura, you go help Mom with the cookin'."

"Oh Harlan, you aren't the boss of me! I don't gotta do what you say."

"Dad says for me to teach the new boy the mornin' chores, now scoot!"

Laura crinkled up her nose at Harlan and stomped her foot on the ground. "Ain't goin'! Can't make me!"

"LAURA ANN! You do as you are told!" her father's voice boomed out of the barn. Laura, red-faced, turned her back on Harlan and Charley and strutted back to the house.

"Follow me, I'll show you how to get the eggs from these old biddies." Harlan was so tall and lanky he could barely stand up straight inside the chicken coop. "These here are the roostin' hens. We keep 'em in the coop when

they's layin' otherwise they find themselves a place some-
wheres else and we gotta go lookin' for 'em. If we don't find
'em, the eggs go all rotten and stink somethin' awful."

"This here is Daisy; she's frisky! Watch she don't peck
ya. Jus' reach right under her nice and easy and grab her
egg. Like so." Harlan pulled out one brown egg and placed
it in a wooden box. Inside the box there were crisscrossed
cardboard squares to hold the eggs upright. Daisy settled
back down with a short squawk. Charley thought, "No big
deal, how hard could it be to pick up some eggs and put
them in a box?"

"Okay, this one here is Bertha. She's a wild one; jus'
reach right under her quick like and grab the egg."

Charley studied Bertha. She clucked contentedly at
him then rearranged herself for a comfortable sit. Charley
lifted his hand in her direction aiming for her nether
regions. Bertha blew up to double her size, stretching her
neck high in the air and shaking her feathers. A high-
pitched, blood-curdling screech pierced the air. Her head
and beak came down on Charley's hand like a hammer
hitting a nail.

"Owww! Hey, you stupid chicken!" Charley pulled his
hand back with lightening speed. He inspected the newly
formed hole in his hand. Bertha's peck had drawn blood.
Her hackles were up! Charley didn't have a chance against
her. He felt stupid in front of Harlan.

"Try it again; can't let a chicken get the best of ya."
Harlan snickered as he grabbed Bertha by the neck right
under her beak so she couldn't peck him. "Take the egg,

quick! She is a mean ol' cluck!" Charley grabbed the prized egg avoiding Bertha's flailing claws. Harlan released his grip, letting go of a disgruntled Bertha.

"Maybe we should let her keep her durn egg!" Charley thought it was mean to take a baby chick from its mother. "Won't it turn into a chick with her sittin' on it?"

"These ain't fertilized eggs; these here are eatin' ones," Harlan answered without expression. Charley wondered how Harlan knew which were eatin' ones and which were hatchin' ones. He decided not to ask. He didn't want to sound stupider than he already felt.

"We got to git a move on. I gotta get the cows milked and out to pasture before breakfast. You finish up with the eggs and then pump a couple a buckets full of water for Ma. Oh ya, she'll be needin' some more wood from the woodpile for the stove, maybe three or four armfuls. Later,

I'll show you how to muck out the stalls and make the slop for the pigs." Harlan disappeared through the door of the chicken coop. Charley looked around, scratched his head and counted the hens. Seven more to go and, oh Lord, he didn't even know their names!

⊶⟶ ⟵⊷

Charley plucked all the eggs with care and placed them one-by-one into the egg carton. He was now in charge of getting the eggs every morning. After he got pecked a few more times, he decided to calm the old hens by singing one of his soothing Irish lullabies. He sang "Tu-ra Lu-ra" staring straight into their beady eyes. The old biddies no longer fought him; instead, they gave up their eggs without a fuss. Feeling proud of his accomplishments, he delivered a full box of unbroken eggs to the kitchen.

"Charleeey, Charleeey! You got a package! It just arrived. What is it Charley? It's so exciting when a package comes! Is it a present?" Laura's eyes danced with anticipation as she pointed to the parcel. Charley put down the eggs on the table next to the package. His heart leapt as he read the carefully written words: Master Charles Kimball Ryan, Care of The Worthington Family, Greene, Maine.

Charley instantly knew what it was. It was his box. He had waited weeks for it. He untied the twine and ripped the brown paper off like it was Christmas morning. His things! He had missed them sorely! They were the only part left of his old world, of his life in Boston.

"Wow, Charley, what ya got in there? Will ya show us?"

Lynette, no longer shy around Charley, had slipped in next to Laura at the kitchen table. "Come on, Charley! We wanna know what you got in there!"

"Hold your horses. I'll show ya, one at a time. I got some pennies in here that Reverend Matthews gave me for giving tours to fancy pants people." The girls watched intently as Charley counted out twelve pennies and placed them in a line on the table. "Sometimes I got me a big ol' penny pickle from Smitty's, but sometimes I saved 'em. Mistress Cummings, the old battleaxe who kept charge of all the keys, would lock them up in my box so nobody stole 'em."

Charley beamed with pride. "This here is my penknife." He held it up in the air to inspect it. He had missed having it in his pocket. He had always felt secure just knowing it was there in case he might need it. A fella never knew when he might need his knife. Charley placed the penknife next to the line of pennies.

Laura let out a sigh of admiration. "I never seen me a prettier penknife than that one." She reached out to stroke its case. "Can you open it, Charley, and show us the blade?"

"Sure, but first I want ta show ya my prize shooter marble. Looky here, ain't she a beauty? She's got all yellow and blue swirlin' inside her. She's my good luck charm; when I shoot with her I always win." Charley held the marble up between his thumb and index finger, allowing the sun to catch it, lighting it up as the early morning rays streamed through the kitchen window.

"It looks like magic, Charley. A magic crystal ball! Will you teach us how to shoot? I ain't ever shot me a marble before!" Lynette was showing her excitement by jumping up and down chanting, "Teach us magic! Teach us magic! Charley's gonna teach us magic!" Laura eagerly joined in and the two girls kicked up their heels dancing giddily around the room.

The bright light shining through the window disappeared as if a sudden cloud had blocked out the sun.

"Give me that!" Granny Rozella screeched as her hand shot into the air grabbing the marble out of Charley's unsuspecting fingers. She scurried out of the room leaving her words ringing in Charley's ears, "There will be no work of the devil in this house! Rotten Irish scum!"

CHAPTER 11

Mows and Ladders

"Mrs. Worthington, ma'am, I need to be askin' you if I could have my shooter marble back. Granny Rozella took it from me for no reason. It was in my box and it belongs to me. I was just showing Laura and Lynette how pretty it was when the sun shone on it and Granny grabs it right outta my hand saying it was the work of the devil or somethin'. Could you get it back for me, please?" Charley couldn't just forget about it; he had to do something, whatever that might be. He would steal it back if he had to. But Laura told him to ask her mother. She said that her ma was kind and that her granny was just plain ol' nuts in the head.

"Yes Charley, I will get the marble back for you. It may take me a little time to wheedle it out of her; old Granny can be cantankerous at times." She reached out and let her hand graze the top of his curls. "Don't worry, it is your belonging and it will be returned to you. Now run along, Pa will be needing your help with the haying today."

Charley felt a little better as he headed toward the hay-loft. He had smoldered all last night worrying about getting his marble back. He even planned that he would take the needle from the old bag's sewing machine and hide it till she gave him his marble back. Why did she have to be so mean? Why did she call him Irish scum? He took a bath once a week like everyone else. The water, so hot from being boiled on the stove, just about scalded the skin right off of him. What did he ever do to her? He couldn't figure it out. Maybe she just was a crazy old bat like Laura said; but still, taking his marble just wasn't right, even if she was missin' some of hers!

"Charley, we need you up in the hay mow now! Grab a pitchfork and get on up there," Mr. Worthington yelled from the top of the hay wagon. The horses were all harnessed up and Harlan was the lucky stiff who got to handle them. Charley had been informed by Laura that that chore was for the oldest boy to do and it was by far the easiest part of all the haying. Harlan walked the team back and forth as Chubb and Maude hauled the pulley rope to lift the hayfork full of hay up to the mow, the place where they stored the hay. Mr. Worthington was in charge of clamping the huge claw into the hay in the wagon. The claw rose high into the air, delivering the hay to the open door of the mow. As soon as the claw was empty of its load, Harlan would walk the horses back to the hay wagon to allow it to dip down once again into the mountain of hay.

Charley was stuck up in the loft alone to deal with the incoming piles of hay. It was hot and sticky up there without even a whisper of a breeze. He itched all over. The prongs of a giant-sized claw sank into the loads of hay that dropped on top of him in the mow. He pitched it over, sweating like a pig, pushing it up under the eaves. He worked till his backbone ached and his nose, allergic to the sweet smell of fresh mown hay, felt like it was on fire. The dust and hay particles settled over him like a haze. He tied a bandana around his face to help filter it. But it still made him sneeze. He craved cold water as if he were on a desert island. His eyes were bloodshot and scratchy by the end of the morning. His hands and face sported red welts that drove him mad with itching. The only possible thing getting him through the day was a vision of the mouth-watering dinner that would be on the table waiting for him. In between the hay stacks, he saw fried chicken covered with gravy and mashed potatoes with puddles of melted butter and he could smell the sweet aroma of steamy cornbread. And the pies, the beautiful glorious pies! Blueberry and raspberry, washed down with ice-cold milk right out of the icebox.

"Hey Charley, need any help? I gotta git out of the kitchen, Ma is workin' my fingers to the bones, chopping and cutting!" Laura swung herself up on the mow in a couple of hops.

"Never mind helpin' me! When is dinner ready? I am gonna die from this hayin'!"

"Ma is whippin' tha potatoes now. Hey, Charley, you ever climb to the top rung and look out the window?" Laura grabbed the steep ladder and began to climb one rung at a time.

"I don't have time, I gotta get this here hay all tucked in flat and even. Your pa will be up here to check after the last load. Gawd, how much hay is left in the wagon? Don't it got no bottom?"

"C'mon, Charley, are ya chicken? Bet I can git up there faster'n you!" Laura scurried up the steps without looking down. Charley stopped to scratch his head; he watched Laura climb. It was awfully high up to the top peak of the barn. He sneezed and wiped his sore nose on his kerchief. He crooked his head back to see if Laura had made it to the top. It made him dizzy to look at her way up there.

"Charley, it is so beautiful! I can see all the way to the neighbor's farm. It's like a doll's house."

"Git yourself down before your pa comes and wallops you one. If ya really want to help, take this here pitchfork and shovel the hay over to the next platform."

"Oh no! Charley, I can't! I looked down and now I am scared ta death. I can't see where my feet are goin'. My hands are all sweatin' and slippery. Will you come up and git me!"

"Laura, you can be a pain! You're a monkey. Now just get yourself down!" Charley looked up to see her face peeking down at him. It was white as a sheet. Her hands were clasped around the top rung and her body was rigid.

"My feet won't work, Charley! I'm stuck here really, *please help me!*" Laura's usual self-assured poise had disappeared.

"Hold on tight and I'll be right there. Don't look down!" Charley threw down the pitchfork and flew up the rungs of the ladder as fast as his legs would take him. He reached Laura and put his right hand on her boot heel. "Okay, Laura, down you come, move this foot to the next rung, I'll guide you. Okay, you got that foot, now move your hand down to match it. Okay, now the other foot,

don't look down! Now keep it going one after the other, one foot then one hand. There you go, you got it, soon we'll be half way down."

"LAURA ANN WORTHINGTON! What are you doing up there on the ladder?" Mr. Worthington's voice boomed across the barn and up to the loft.

Charley winced. "Sorry, sir, I was just helping Laura get down; she got up there and got herself scared."

"Never mind excuses. Get yourselves down and wash up for dinner. Ma's been waiting on you to finish up and here you two are playing games. Laura Ann, you know you are not allowed on that ladder. Young man, when you are haying, you are part of the team, there is no time for jollying around. After you have your dinner you and Laura can clean out the chicken coop."

Laura groaned out loud as they finished the climb down to the hayloft. Charley was exhausted as they entered the kitchen. His stomach growled as soon as he saw the heaping piles of delicious homemade food.

"Here is your marble, Charley!" Mrs. Worthington held out her hand; the marble lay in her plump palm. Charley wrapped his fingers around it and held on tight.

"Thanks, Mrs. Worthington!"

"Would you sing for us tonight after supper? I have tuned up the piano and our neighbors, the Andersons, are coming to visit."

"Sure, I'll sing for you, Mrs. Worthington, anytime."

Harlan dug out a huge clump of mashed potatoes from the crockery bowl and slapped them onto his plate. He snickered. "Ha, ha, sing for your supper; that's a good one! Don't think it will pay for the food ya put in your belly!"

"Harlan, mind your manners! Charley's worked hard at the haying and he is a growing boy, just like you," Mrs. Worthington bristled at Harlan. Everyone at the table grew quiet as Mr. Worthington began to say the grace before the meal.

⋆⇒ ⇐⋆

After stuffing themselves with dinner Laura and Charley walked over to the chicken coop. Charley was humming the tune of "Danny Boy." He wished they were on their way to jump in the pond down the road. After a refreshing dip, he could try his hand at catching a fish or take a snooze under the big oak tree on this stifling, sticky, August afternoon.

"Yuck, I thought the hayin' was bad, but this is the worst ever. These here chickens are disgustin'! How come they don't do their business outside?" Charley scraped the shovel across the wooden floor. "What is it made of, cement? I can't chip it off. These durn feathers stick to it; yuck, it smells durn disgustin'!"

"Charley you're so funny! Just heave all that stuff outside. I got the sprayer for mites, we gotta do the walls and the floor."

"What's a mite? Is it like lice?"

"They are miserable creatures that drive the poor hens next ta crazy from itchin'."

"Gawd, poor Minnie had lice in her hair."

"Your sister?" Laura asked as she fiddled with the sprayer.

"My little sister, she went to live with some fancy pants folks in Boston." Charley frowned not wanting to think about Minnie. "Might as well spray me while you're at it! I'm itchin' worse than them chickens!" Charley turned his back on Laura as he heaved a load of straw, feathers and chicken manure out the door.

Laura squeezed the sprayer covering Charley's whole backside with mite spray.

"Hey, watcha doin'?"

"You told me to spray ya!" Laura gave Charley another playful spritz covering the tops of his boots.

"That does it! You're in big trouble now!" Charley sprang toward her in an attempt to get the sprayer. Laura fell backwards, landing on several of the roostin' hens. The hens screeched and feathers flew in every direction. Nests were abandoned as the escapees ran out a small, hen-sized door to the back of the coop. The hens, enclosed within the framework of chicken wire, ran around in circles squawking their heads off. You'd think someone was after them with an axe and dinner on their minds. Only Bertha remained. She pompously strutted up to Charley and, giving him a sideways withering look, proceeded to peck him hard, smack on the toe of his boot.

Laura gave way to a big belly laugh. "Good work, Charley; you got all the hens out 'cepten' Bertha! Now we can finish up with some fresh new straw for them settin' ladies!"

"Okay, then let's beat it down to the pond before

supper chores." Charley could already feel the cool water streaming down his itchy face and arms. He needed to cool down bad. He had to get the itchin' to stop before he could sing tonight!

Laura grabbed some clean bedding, threw it on the roosts, and scrambled out of the chicken coop calling, "Last one in is a rotten egg!"

⟶ CHAPTER 12 ⟵

Fallen Apples!

"Today is the day for Charley to learn to milk the ladies," Mr. Worthington announced as he rose from his chair to his full height of six feet two inches tall. Charley, feeling smaller than ever, had been dreading those words. He didn't feel real easy around the big animals like the cows and the horses. The cows acted gentle and dumb, but their bulk seemed immense to Charley. And it made him nervous that the horses always had one back hoof poised and ready to kick him in the shins. Now Laura, she never acted afraid of the ladies, she just slapped them on the behind and told them to git!

"Well, sir, I sure am hoping they like me," Charley answered as he reluctantly pulled on his wool jacket. It was getting crisp these early September mornings. You could see your breath coming out of your mouth like the smoke of George's cigar. He wished he could stay in the warm kitchen and help with the cookin' and get another piano lesson from Mrs. Worthington. Last evening after supper she had played for him while he sang some of his old songs. She taught him the chords on the piano to go along with them. It was great fun except for the dark shadow Granny Rozella cast, sitting and sewing in the same room. She sniped at him under her breath, muttering mean things the whole dang time he sang.

"Sings like an Irish devil. Can't get a moment's peace . . . Irish trash living in our house . . . No more than a shiftless boarder." It was being called a boarder that cut into his spirits the most. No one else in the room seemed to notice or pay her any mind, but Charley felt every dart she threw his way.

Charley ran his fingers through his hair as if to tame it, then slapped his cap on his head. The last thing he wanted to do was to try to squeeze some milk out of a big old smelly cow. But he followed Mr. Worthington and Harlan out the door and down the path to the barn.

"It is not a major accomplishment to milk a cow. It is as simple as one, two, three. Wash up first, then grab yourself a stool and sit down by her side, out of the way of her hooves and tail."

Charley did as he was told, sitting far enough away so that no part of the cow could possibly come in contact with him. "Move in closer, boy. You can't milk yourself a cow from across the barn."

Charley scooted himself and the stool in closer. The cow's head was secured between two upright boards, and she had plenty of hay to eat. He could hear the cow chewing her cud. Hot breath escaped from her wide nostrils. Flies buzzed around her; she swished her tail, chasing them away, only to have them return again. He glanced under her wide belly, where a bloated udder and four faucets hung down. He moaned, "Oh shoot, I can't do this, it's disgustin'!"

Mr. Worthington, ignoring Charley's comment, took a wet rag and rubbed it over the faucets and udder of the cow, removing mud and barnyard dirt. He then went to the washbasin, rolled up his sleeves and lathered his hands with soap. Charley couldn't stop staring at the enormous size of Mr. Worthington's hands. Harlan, two cows down the row, was producing rapid squirting noises into the tin milk pail, jangling Charley's nerves even more.

"Now Charley, rub your hands together to get some heat in them. Cows don't cotton to cold fingers." Mr. Worthington, first rubbing his hands together, sat on the stool clenching the waiting bucket between his knees. "You take the teat between your thumb and first finger, like so. Tug downward, wrapping all your other fingers around the teat with just enough pressure until the milk is squeezed from the teat. Make sure you aim into the bucket. The more relaxed you are the more relaxed the cow will be. Now pull in closer and give her a try."

Charley set his stool up to the side of the cow as close as he dared. The cow smelled earthy like salt, sweat and manure. She stopped chewing and turned her head in her stanchion to look back at Charley. To him, her eyes were enormous brown pools of fear. She swished her tail in agitation. Mr. Worthington, sitting on his stool next to Charley, grabbed hold of the flailing cow's tail. Charley gulped some air and swallowed hard. He picked up the pail and clamped it between his knees. He reached his hand under the cow until his fingers came in contact with the teat. He encircled it with his thumb and first finger. It felt strangely soft and firm at the same time. Sweat poured down the side of his face and down his back. He wrapped the rest of his

fingers around his target and squeezed hard, pulling downward. The cow bellowed. Charley released his grip on the teat, yanking his hand away from the cow so vehemently that he fell backwards off his stool landing on his behind. There he sat, legs splayed out on the barn floor, utterly bewildered.

Harlan stuck his head out from behind his cow and, in Charley's opinion, laughed harder than he needed to. Mr. Worthington just said, "Get back up on your stool, Charley; you're going to milk this cow today!"

The whole cow milking experience turned out to be exasperating. Charley pulled and squeezed the uncooperative teat till his arms and fingers were numb. The pinging sound of milk squirting steady into the tin bucket never rewarded his ears. He managed to get a few slippery squirts into the bucket before the beast shifted her weight knocking Charlie off balance. The bucket and its meager contents fell to the ground. Then the cow, as if to make Charley look even worse, placed her rear hoof smack into the spilt milk.

"Dang! Hoof in the spilt milk! Shoot! Now I gotta start all over again!" By now he was ready to kick both the cow and the bucket! Then Harlan had to come along, carrying a full bucket of milk. He glanced down at the pitiful puddle of milk under Charley's cow.

"Hey, Charley, you should stick with the chickens. You're good doin' girls' work."

Charley fumed to himself, "One of these days he's gonna get a knuckle sandwich right in the chops."

A short while later, Charley poured his minor offering of milk into the separator. Mr. Worthington and Harlan had made fast work of finishing the rest of the ladies, ten in all. They poured bucket after bucket of foaming milk into the tank. Charley got assigned the boring job of turning the hand crank that separated the milk from the cream. He thought his arm was going to fall off. Harlan and Mr. Worthington carried the milk jugs and cream to the icehouse. Charley, left behind, was told to scrub the machine until it was spotless and ready for the next milking. He wondered why anyone would ever think of taking up dairy farming!

⊶⊜ ⊜⊷

"Charley, I'd like you to keep a check on the cows. The apples have started to fall and the cows eat them like candy. If they eat too many it gives 'em a bad bellyache and can make 'em real sick. The apples that are falling are in the far north pasture. Keep 'em down in the south pasture." Mr. Worthington spoke while he harnessed up Maud and Chubb. "Harlan and I are goin' into town to get us some supplies. I'll get your letters posted."

"Yes, sir! Thanks for taking my letters. Don't worry a bit about the ladies, I will check on 'em. If they get near those apples, I'll just slap them on their bottoms and tell them to git!" Charley chuckled as he pushed his cap to the back of his head. He wasn't scared of the cows so much anymore. He did his regular share, or almost, of the milking most every day. He couldn't beat Harlan's speed, but that was okay. What bothered him most was that Harlan always had to get under his skin and call him "the boarder." And it irritated him no end when Harlan continued to mock him that he should be milking the chickens instead of the cows, because they were more his size. But, ha! He showed Harlan the other day when he won six cats-eye marbles from him. That lucky shooter marble still worked like magic. Harlan turned sour and kept accusing Charley of cheating. He sure was a sore loser.

Charley rubbed his stomach, it felt full and content after his big breakfast of griddlecakes smothered in buttery maple syrup and finished off with crunchy fried pork rinds. Mrs. Worthington sure was a great cook; her food was even better than the Home's meals, and those, he thought, were pretty durn good. He could still eat like a horse. Sometimes he would flex his upper arm muscles when no one was around. They had grown strong and hard since he came to the farm those few months ago. He added an inch or two to his height. His work pants didn't scrape the ground like they did when they were new.

He snapped out of his thoughts when he heard Laura approaching. "Hey, Charley! Guess what? Ma let me out of the kitchen. Wahoo! Shoot, my hands are all red and burnin' from doin' the dishes with that awful soap. Ma makes it from pork fat and ashes; sure don't know how rubbin' somethin' made from pork fat and ashes on dishes can make 'em clean." Laura held out her hands for Charley to inspect.

"Those hands of yours need to go fishin', that'll make 'em feel durn better. Pond water will wash all that greasy pork fat off 'em." Charley's eyes shone with the prospect of a day just lounging and maybe catchin' a fish and gettin' sleepy under the old oak tree.

"That's a deal! If you grab us some poles, I'll get Ma to pack us a picnic lunch of ham sandwiches and some apple pie for dessert!" Laura skipped back toward the kitchen door.

"Apples! I gotta check the cows to make sure they ain't near the apples. Durn it! It could take me all mornin' to move them stupid cows," Charley said to himself. The door had banged closed behind Laura as she entered the kitchen. "The cows are fine," he thought. "How could a couple a' apples hurt 'em anyways? I'll check them on the way back from fishing before Mr. Worthington gets back from town." Charley rambled into the back shed and found two fishing poles and all the gear they needed in a woven basket hanging on the wall. He slung the poles over his shoulder and the basket over his arm. He rushed to meet Laura, whistling a happy-go-lucky tune.

Laura showed up with a picnic basket in one hand and her rifle in the other. "I got my rifle to take along in case we see any varmints! Pa wants me ta git that fat old woodchuck cuz he's been eatin' up Ma's kitchen garden real bad." Lynette followed close behind Laura. "Ma says Lynnie has to come, too!" Laura crossed her eyes and stuck out her tongue at her sister, who twirled around in a circle, ignoring the fact that maybe she wasn't welcome.

Charley, attacked by a nagging conscience said, "Wait here just a minute. I gotta go see if the cows have wandered off anywhere near them apples. I'll just climb the ladder to the little room at the top of the barn. I should be able to see all the way to the north pasture from way up there." Charley, with lightning speed, climbed the two flights leading up to the third story topmost ladder. He slowed with caution as he climbed the steep ladder to the top. Ah ha! No sign of the cows anywhere near the apples. He counted eight of the black and white Holsteins; they were all settled in near the brook by the south pasture. The other two, he figured, would be somewhere near the others.

"It's okay to go, the ladies ain't anywhere's near them apples." Charley and the two girls headed off across the fields toward the pond. It was one of those days in early September that the sun sparkled through the leaves of the trees and the breeze came fresh and clear.

They devoured their lunch as soon as Laura pulled it out of the basket, and then Charley set to his first try at fishing. The afternoon went by lazily without the slightest tug on his line. He had to retie a new worm when they seemed to slip off of his hook for no good reason. Charley started to doze in the shade of the giant oak tree when he got a pull, followed by a good-sized yank! Laura jumped into action screaming, "Holy macaroni! Charley, don't let him get away." He reeled in with all his might but it tugged and fought back ferociously. Charley held on, his arms and shoulders straining in the battle. The water splashed up and all around as the wild thing flapped back and forth fighting for its life. With all the strength that Charley could muster he took his final stand and reeled in his catch, lifting it high up out of the water! The long squirming creature dangling on the end of his line was the ugliest fish he had ever seen!

"Shoot! Laura, you ever seen something like this before?"

"You caught yourself an eel! Yes, sirree, that there is an eel for sure." Laura danced up and down clapping her hands, excited to see his catch. Lynette, horrified, hid behind the tree.

"An eel? It is durn disgustin'!" Charley held it as far away from himself as the pole would allow.

"Let's take it home! We can put it in the water trough; the cows won't mind, don't ya think?" Laura watched delighted as the eel writhed and swung from Charley's pole. Charley had no plans on taking that eel anywhere. He just wanted to get it off his line as quick as he could.

"We ain't takin' this ugly eel nowheres! This here one is going right back where he comes from, just like them rats in Boston. Here, Laura, hold the pole. I'll cut the line with my knife." Laura grabbed onto the pole with both hands. Charley dug into his pocket, pulled out his penknife and clicked it open.

"I could smack it against the tree, then we could give it to Ma to cook for supper," Laura offered.

"No! I ain't never eating some ugly old snake!" Lynette cried from her safe hiding spot.

Charley swiftly cut the eel free from the pole and watched as it splashed back into the pond water. "There, now we got to git back, time to check on them cows!"

Charley whistled a soft Irish lullaby as he, Laura and Lynette packed up their picnic supplies and started out on their trek across the fields.

"It's great to be free on such a grand day as this one, Charley. Tomorrow we're back to sitting upright in hard desks and wearin' shoes again." Laura stopped dead in her tracks. Lynette and Charley froze, too. There it came again, a wailing horrible sound.

Charley whispered, "What is it?"

"Maybe a bear got into the pigpen and the hog gave him a toss with his tusks." Laura slid her fingers down the barrel of her gun. "Good thing I got my rifle with me!"

"You ain't gonna kill no bear with that bitsy rifle of yourn!" Lynette pointed her finger at her sister.

"Wait a minute, that ain't no bear. Bears don't bellow!" Laura looked at Charley, her eyes wide with fear. "Shoot! That there sounds like a cow screamin' its head off!"

"Oh Gawd! The apples!" Charley dropped the fishing rods and broke into a full sprint. He had never heard the likes of it in his life. Not even a trolley car wheels screeching to a sudden stop on a steel track could compare to this! Laura kept up full steam behind him. Lynette found herself left behind with the fishing rods and picnic basket.

As Charley and Laura approached the scene, Charley's heart sunk to his feet. Mr. Worthington was already there. One of the cows raised her head and let out a pitiful moan. Mr. Worthington, his back to Laura and Charley, bent over her wiping her brow. Charley slowed his pace. He was afraid to face Mr. Worthington. Laura ran to her father.

"What's the matter, Pa? Did the cows get into the apples?"

Mr. Worthington turned to answer her when he saw Charley. "Where have you been? You were to check on the cows. I told you not to let them get into the apples. You didn't do your job, boy. These two are mighty sick. They must have eaten a bushel of the fallen crab apples. We got us back from town to hear 'em bellowing like their bellies had burst. Harlan's gone to fetch the vet."

"Sir, I checked them this morning and they weren't anywhere near the north pasture." Charley tried to control the shaking in his voice.

"This morning was this morning; this afternoon's this afternoon!" Mr. Worthington turned his attention back to the ailing cows. Charley pulled his cap down over his forehead, shielding his eyes and himself beneath it.

It took forever for Harlan and the vet to come. Charley searched the road for the familiar silhouettes of Maude and Chubb. Finally they arrived! Charley prayed, please, please, let him save the cows!

The vet hopped down from the wagon holding onto a black bag. He nodded at Mr. Worthington and set to examining the sick cows. He ran his hand up and down their sides placing his stethoscope on their bellies. Then with a crease down his forehead, he cleared his throat and said, "We have to cut their stomachs, I am afraid there is no other way. This is a dangerous procedure, but the gas has built up so much that their bellies will rupture, and that will surely kill them."

Charley, with Laura beside him, stood stock still in

horror. It had to be a bad dream. Laura opened her mouth to speak but nothing came out.

"Okay, Doc, you know best." Mr. Worthington wiped his forehead with the sleeve of his coat and stared at the lamenting cows. He didn't speak to Laura or Charley. Charley felt guilty, guilty to the core. He had failed miserably.

"Edwin, I don't know if the children should be here watching this procedure. It's a mighty messy one." The doctor gestured toward Charley and Laura.

"Go on with it. They can watch; they just might be learning a mighty hard lesson today."

The doctor took out a scalpel the size of a small slicing knife. With one quick motion he reached under the cow's belly and made a slit. The sound that came out of that cow was absolutely terrifying. Rumbling thunder! A ripping explosion of gas filled the air!

Then, as quick as he cut the first one, he cut the second. Both cows lay on their sides stunned, eyes rolling back in their heads. The doctor examined the incisions and cleaned them with a red liquid from a bottle he pulled out of his bag. He then laced a long thin needle, just like the sewing needles Granny Rozella used, with a piece of what looked like fishing line. The cows seemed to understand his working on them was for their own good. The first cow's moans had lessened. But the second cow continued a sorrowful tune. Charley wished he could take the cow's pain away.

"I think we have done all we can do; now it is up to

them. Let them rest. It will be best to get them back into the barn by nightfall. They'll be plenty sore for a day or two so be careful when you milk them." The doctor piled all his tools back into his bag. After wiping his hands on a clean cloth, he shook Mr. Worthington's hand.

"Thanks, Doc. We appreciate your help. Harlan will drive you home." Mr. Worthington walked alone back to the house never once looking back at Charley and Laura.

CHAPTER 13

One Room School House

Charley was lying in bed when the rifle shot cracked through the air. He buried his face into his pillow, using his fists to cover his ears. He never dreamt that Mr. Worthington would have to shoot it. The kitchen door whined then slammed shut with a bang. The shuffle of Mr. Worthington's boots echoed in Charley's ears as he crossed the worn floorboards of the kitchen. He heard a heartfelt sigh as Mr. Worthington sat down heavily in his kitchen chair. Charley could picture Mr. Worthington's stern countenance as he faced his wife across the table. Then Charley heard the awful words. "Mary, the cow is dead. It wasn't a pretty sight; poor thing was sufferin' something terrible. I figure she had ruptured before the doc could help her. I had to let the old girl go. The second one will make it through okay, if she makes it through this night."

"Oh, Edwin, I am so sorry about the cow! Charley will feel terrible when he hears." Charley pictured her wringing her hands then wiping her eyes with her apron.

"Charley? Charley?" His fist pounded down hard on the wooden table. "That boy *ought* to feel terrible. It is his fault that the cow is dead. It was his job to keep the cows from getting to the apples. He proved himself to be untrustworthy. Mary, I am not at all certain that boy belongs here."

"Oh, but Edwin. He didn't mean it to happen. He has so much to learn about farming and animals. He has only been here for a short summer. It is not like he grew up living on a farm like Harlan and Laura."

Mr. Worthington interrupted his wife, "Laura should have known better!"

But she continued on, determined to make her point. "The poor boy grew up on city streets. He was abandoned by his father and orphaned by his mother. He had no supervision and wasn't taught properly how to be responsible for anyone let alone an animal. I think we should give him something to take care of by himself. Something all his own, maybe Doll the old mare?"

"Mary! What are you thinking of? You don't reward a child with the care of an animal after he has caused one to die!"

The words spoken ricocheted in Charley's brain. He wanted to roll over and die. How could he face any of them? How could he say good morning and go out to help milk the cows when there was one cow less? Charley wished he had never come to this farm. He wasn't cut out to be a farmer. Mistress Renée was right; he should have stayed at the Home and sung with the choir, at least he knew how to do that. Maybe he was like his father, he could sing and dance but he couldn't hold down a decent job. The night proved to be unending for Charley. He wrestled with his blankets and punched his pillow. He broke out in a hot sweat and threw the covers on the floor. All he could think about was the cows with their awful moans, and the gruesome look of pain in their bulging eyes haunted him.

When he awoke his eyes were almost swollen shut and his body ached as if he had been tossed in the air by a bull. He heard familiar bustling sounds in the kitchen, ones that he had allowed to lure him from his slumbers most mornings. He pulled his covers back up over himself and listened as Mrs. Worthington poked sticks in the stove and scratched the match to start the fire. Next, would come the clink of the black iron kettle being set upon the back burner to boil. The whistle of the kettle was often his alarm clock. But this morning, these sounds were not comforting. Yesterday's events remained fresh and raw in his mind. He wished them all away but they remained, hovering around him no matter which way he tried to make his mind go. He must write another letter to George today. He must tell George he wasn't cut out to be a farmer and that he would, somehow, find his way back to Boston!

Laura stuck her head in his room, her face beaming with excitement "Hey, Charley! Are you up? Today is the first day of school! Hurry up, I'll race ya out ta the barn."

"Ya. You go along. I'm not racing this morning." He dragged himself out of bed, rubbed his bleary eyes, and pulled his chore clothes on piece by piece, wishing he was in another place, any place, but here on this farm.

Chores were finished in a bustle of activity and Charley managed to make it through, avoiding Harlan completely. Mr. Worthington had awoken early; both he and the dead cow were gone. Mrs. Worthington provided Charley with a hearty breakfast of boiled oatmeal. He mashed it around with his spoon, but he could not eat. He excused himself and changed into clean clothes for the first day of school. He trudged behind Laura and Lynette. Laura, refusing to allow Charley to be unfriendly, slowed herself down to his pace and babbled at him all the way to school. She talked about the teacher and told him which kids were nice and which weren't. Charley barely heard a word she said the whole mile hike to the schoolhouse. When they arrived Charley didn't want to enter. But Laura gave him a playful shove and he found himself inside with all the other kids.

"Good morning, class! It is wonderful to see my pupils

again after such a nice long summer. I see we have some new faces too! For those of you I haven't met yet, you may call me Miss Peterson. Now, I would like the new students to come forward to the front of the class. The rest of you may take your assigned seats. You each have a new journal at your desk. I want you to write about the most meaningful day of your summer." Miss Peterson smiled as she spoke.

Charley thought she looked friendly enough. She was young, probably about the same age as Mistress Renée. She wasn't as pretty, but she wasn't what you would call ugly either. She wore spectacles that sat pinched forward on her thin nose. A black belt was cinched tight around her waist and her long skirt flowed to the floor tickling the tops of her boots. A cameo pin was attached to the center of her blouse just below a lace-filled collar. Her light brown hair was pulled back into a round tight bun.

Her gray-green eyes shone clear and trustworthy as she spoke to Charley. "Please tell me your name, how old you are and what schooling you have had."

"My name is Charley Kimball Ryan. I am twelve years old, soon to be thirteen, and I have gone to school in Boston. Last time I went to school I was in grade seven."

"Welcome Charley! Seeing as you are the only new student that is not beginning first grade, I would like you to take some simple tests. That way I will know where to place you in the class. Why don't you sit up front for now? There are only three short tests: math, reading and Maine history." She had a reassuring pleasantness about her that made him feel at ease. Laura had told him over and over how super a teacher she was. He had to agree that she seemed okay by him, so far.

"Math is first. Do all the problems as well as you can. If they get too difficult, stop. Raise your hand and I will give you the next test. Now all you other people get to work writing in your journals. I will be calling on you to read what you have written." She nodded at Charley to begin, and then spread her arms out wide to gather her newest little ones just starting their first year of school.

"My new pupils! You must be so happy you are now old enough to come to our Mountain School House. After you tell me your names, and a little about yourselves, I will pass to you some new crayons and a big piece of paper so you can draw your most favorite summer day."

The schoolhouse buzzed with activity. Charley looked up and down the rows of students; it was clear to him that he and Harlan were the two oldest boys. Laura had told him that Harlan had already turned thirteen. He wondered which grade Harlan was in. He hoped that they weren't going to be together for any lessons or, even worse, have to sit next to each other. He got his mind back on task and finished the test quickly. He raised his pencil in the air and said, "Ma'am, I am finished with the math."

"Very good, Charley. I am glad that you stopped rather than try to go on to problems you can't do yet." She picked up the test, glancing at the front and back of both pages. "Why, Charley, you have finished all the problems, very good. I will check them while you work on the reading comprehension test."

In less than twenty minutes, Charley had his pencil up in the air. "Ma'am, I have answered all the questions." Charley stuck his pencil into his thick curls, turning it like a screw so that when he let it go it spun around like a pinwheel. Laura, who looked up from her journal writing, laughed out loud. Several others joined in. Pencils were being twisted into braids and stuck behind ears every which way. Laughter rose to a high pitch. Charley was pleased that the kids in the school were eager for jollying around. All but Harlan, who didn't even look up let alone crack a smile.

"Charley, that is quite enough," Miss Peterson spoke firmly. "This group, as you can see, is easily amused. Please, class! Take the pencils out of your hair and ears. Now Charley, here is your last test, as soon as you finish you may join the rest of the class."

"Last one done, Miss Peterson. This here one wasn't so easy 'cause I don't know much about Maine history. I mostly know about Boston and the Revolutionary War with England and the founding fathers: Washington, Jefferson and Adams. And I know about Paul Revere and the battle at Concord and the Boston Tea Party and Independence Day July 4, 1776." Charley gave her a winning smile.

"Well, Charley Kimball Ryan, it looks like you have passed the first two tests with flying colors. Don't worry about the Maine state test, it seems like you have a good handle on American history. I think you will be best placed in eighth grade. That means that you and Harlan are my two eighth graders. You will have to work hard together! This is the year you need to prepare for the test to go on to high school in Lewiston.

"Oh, ma'am, I don't think I'll be goin' to any high school. I only need to stay in school till I'm fourteen."

"I see. Well, Charley, if you aren't going on to high school, tell me what is it that you like to do best?" Miss Peterson had a concerned look on her face and a slight furrow appeared between her brows.

"I like to sing, ma'am; that is what I do best of all!"

"Well now, is that true? Then we must hear you sing! The Christmas play tryouts will be coming up right after potato harvest. The lead role is a gallant toy soldier and he needs a strong voice."

The teacher walked over to an upright piano, uncovered it and plinked down on several keys. "Hmm, this is still in reasonable tune. Let's give it a try, Charley, come over here while the others finish up their journals. What song do you sing best?" She pulled out a stool and sat down poised and ready to play.

"'Danny Boy,' is my favorite. My best friend in Boston's name is Big Dan and I used ta sing it for him all the time." Charley ran his hand through his hair, he could feel his cheeks burning. He wasn't so sure this was the best time for him to try out. He looked over to Harlan. His head was bent down and his pencil waggled back and forth across his paper, but it didn't look like he was writing anything down.

"Do you know the chords?" Her fingers were tapping the tops of the keys eager to begin.

"Yes, ma'am, Mrs. Worthington showed me how to play the chords." Charley, without any effort, placed his fingers on the keys and punched out the chords to the first and then the second verse. As he did, he sang along to keep himself on track.

"Class, I think we may have found our lead for the play this year, even before potato harvest!" Then Miss Peterson lowered her voice to a whisper and spoke directly to Charley. "Charley, you are very talented. Do you know that I teach piano lessons every day after school? Would you like to stay today and work on your song 'Danny Boy'?"

Charley whispered back to her. "Well, ma'am, I sure would 'cept I gotta go home to do my farm chores. You see, I am living at the Worthington Farm and I gotta do my share. I messed up bad yesterday and they lost a cow 'cause of me. I feel real bad; I can't ask for any time off. I gotta make it up to them; either that, or I should just quit and go back to my brother in Boston." Charley looked away from the teacher feeling embarrassed that he had told her too much. He tugged at his hair wishing his curls would for once straighten out and lie flat on his head like the other boys' hair.

"That's okay, Charley; sounds like you have a lot going on in your life. But I think that, if we try, we will be able to find a way to get some music lessons in during class. Seeing as you have scored higher than anyone ever has before on the placement tests!" Her face was soft and kind, but her eyes radiated intense determination.

Miss Peterson called the class to attention asking for a volunteer to read their journal entry. Laura raised her hand shaking it up and down frantically until the teacher called on her. She stood up in the aisle next to her desk and read aloud, "The day that Charley came to our farm." She smiled over at Charley who was wishing he could evaporate into thin air. Laura continued on reading her entry, about how Charley came to Maine on the railroad train, and how he sang with a choir, and that her mama picked him from all the kids. Mama said she wanted, "The boy that sang alone." And how Charley came home with them that very night.

Harlan was looking a little green around the edges. Charley saw him fold up his journal and jam it deep into his desk. When the teacher rang the afternoon bell, Harlan slid out of his seat without a word. Some of the younger boys gathered around him like he was a hero. As Charley stepped out of the schoolhouse he heard Harlan announce, "That ain't no brother of mine! He's just a stupid boarder. Ma feels sorry for him, 'cause he's an orphan. Pa says he don't earn his keep. Just yesterday he killed one of our cows! C'mon, let's get out of here!"

Laura popped out of the schoolhouse. "Hey, Charley! Will you walk home with Lynnie and me? Harlan's run off with the boys. He sure was in an ornery old mood today. Don't know what's gettin' his goat? He used ta always walk us home from school."

"I think I know what's getting' his goat!" Charley pulled his cap down tight on his forehead and frowned. Laura looked at him with a puzzled expression on her face.

"What, Charley? Tell me? What's gettin' his durn goat?"

"Me!"

⟿ CHAPTER 14 ⟸

Pulling Whiskers

Dear George,

Have you heard from Pa? Let me know as soon as you hear from him. I got to tell you, George, I am not a farmer. I have to get back to Boston. Things here are not good. A cow died because it ate apples and got a bad bellyache and it is my fault. Mrs. Worthington, the ma, is nice and makes great pies, but Granny calls me mean Irish names.

Harlan is the only boy here. He is just a year older than me by a month. He always makes me feel stupid when it comes to farm chores. I think he hates me and wants me to go away. The schoolteacher is nice but she put me in the same grade with him. He does not look at me or talk to me at school, he acts like I am not even there. He calls me a stupid boarder!

I got the lead role in the Christmas play because I can sing, but that just made Harlan madder. I think that is why he keeps giving me the worst chores, like every morning I have to muck out the stalls for the cows and the horses which means pitching out all the stinking manure then pitching in the clean straw. By the time I'm done I smell like a cow and it's time to go to school! Then he has me mix the slop feed for the hogs. *Hogs are big fat ornery old things that roll around in the mud. One day when I went to feed them, the big old hog charged me with its tusks. They are sharp teeth that stick out mean. It sliced through my pant leg, missing cutting my leg by a hair. Laura screamed for me to get out of the pen. She showed me how to pour the slop over the top of the fence into the trough so you don't get gored.*

Laura is about the only thing that is good here. She is a girl but she acts like a boy. We go fishing and I taught her how to shoot marbles. She has her own single shot twenty-two rifle. She is the best shot around here. She shoots mostly varmints like rabbits and hangs them up till her ma skins and cooks them up in a stew.

Did you get to visit Minnie? Is she still happy with the fancy pants Boston people? Tell her and Clarence to write me. Are they working Clarence to death on that farm? Do you ever see Big Dan? He hangs around down by the wharf a lot. I need to come back to Boston real soon. The Home was going to send someone to come and see how I am doing. Well I have not seen one person come yet! Not even one letter from Mistress Renée. That's all for now. Write if you hear from Pa!

  Your brother,
  Charley

Charley read his letter to himself and then folded it over several times and tucked it into the envelope that Mrs. Worthington had placed on top of his chest of drawers. He wrote George's name and the address he had given him the night before they went to the Home. Charley licked the edge of the paper and rubbed his fingers across it to make sure it would stick. He sure wouldn't want Mr. Worthington or Harlan to see the insides of it when they took it to town. Charley wondered if it might be possible for him to go along instead of Harlan. Then he shook his head no; Harlan would never give up his seat next to his father! Never to him, anyways!

Charley walked into the kitchen and placed his letter face up on the table. Mrs. Worthington was busy canning jars of applesauce. She looked up from her chores and saw that Charley had finished his letter. "Well Charley, that is good of you to write your brother. Mr. Worthington and Harlan are going to make a trip to town for some supplies; I will make sure the letter goes with them. Now sit down and have some of my applesauce. I like to make it before Christmas; it makes the house smell like cinnamon and spices."

"Thank you, Mrs. Worthington. That's mighty kind of you." Charley felt at home around her. He liked the warmth in the kitchen and the way she hummed while she worked and minded the baby at the same time. Charley smiled, amused by the antics of the baby, who was hitting the bottom of a pan with a long wooden spoon. Then she'd stop and lick it. Charley figured the spoon must have been used to stir the sauce and still had a lingering sweet taste clinging to it. The image of the child and mother took him to a place long ago, a kitchen with a mother and a baby playing on the floor.

"I am so much looking forward to the play this year with you being the star and all." Mrs. Worthington dished him up a big bowl of warm spicy sauce with chunks of apples floating on the top.

"I ain't no star, Mrs. Worthington; I just like to sing like my pa did. He sang all the time." Charley took a big chunk of bread, but before he put it in his mouth he asked, "I was wondering, do you think Harlan is mad at me 'cause I got the lead part in the Christmas play?"

"It is funny you should ask that, Charley. Harlan, he keeps to himself, so I can't always tell what upsets him, or what makes him happy either. He has been more quiet than usual and I just haven't been able to figure out what's going on with him. He sure isn't like Laura, a body knows what is going on with her everyday because it all comes out her mouth!"

"What comes out of whose mouth?" Laura stuck her head into the kitchen with an impish grin. Without waiting for an answer she directed her attention towards Charley.

"Hey, Charley, can you help me with my lines for the play? I can't get them straight in my head. The lines for my poem bobble about in my brain and come out at the wrong places."

"Sure, I'll help; we can practice together. Let me grab my script." Charley stuck the bread in his mouth and disappeared into his bedroom. When he returned, he found Laura in the parlor pushing the chairs to one side of the room. Charley joined in, helping her to make a proper stage.

The only thing they didn't dare move was Granny Rozella's sewing table.

Lynette bounded into the parlor. "Hey, can I practice too?"

"But you only have one line. All you say is, 'Meow, Meow! I am the cat.' So say it, then scat!" Laura brushed her away with her hand.

"No! Let me stay or I'll tell Granny!" Lynette stomped her foot down hard.

"You tell Granny and we'll hang you upside down by your ankles and tie your pigtails to the tree stump!" Laura snickered at her.

Charley stepped in between the two sisters. "Lynette can stay and watch; we need to get used ta people watchin'!" Charley scratched his head with his knuckles and then tucked the stray ends of his curls behind his ears. The short haircut from the Home was long gone. Then with a devilish twinkle in his eye he bent over and cackled like a wicked old witch. He walked back and forth inspecting the two girls from a bent position mumbling to himself loud enough for them to hear.

"Ah, the dirty Irish scum has come to tarnish our blessed home," he cackled. Laura and Lynette clapped their hands, showing their pleasure at Charley's antics.

Then, Charley stopped in his tracks, and looking at Laura, tugged on a few make-believe hairs on his chin. Laura broke into contagious giggles and Lynette joined in. Charley furrowed his eyebrows and stuck out his chin as far as it would go. Then, with an exaggerated movement, he pinched his fingers tightly on one invisible hair. He yanked hard. You could almost hear the pop of the offending hair as he extracted it from his chin. The girls burst into fits of laughter. Laura flopped on the floor pounding her fists on the floorboards, begging Charley to stop. Lynette, unable to contain herself, fell into a swoon, landing on top of Laura.

Suddenly, from behind Charley, a hand attached to a long black sleeve grabbed his ear. "I caught you!" screeched Granny Rozella. "You devil! You come with me to see my son; he will know what to do with a street beggar!" As she spoke she twisted Charley's ear so hard that he thought she might unscrew it right out of his head. Laura and Lynette popped up like jack-in-the-boxes. They brushed themselves off, straightening their dresses, trying to make themselves presentable. Granny Rozella led Charley by his ear out of the parlor and through the kitchen to the mudroom beyond. There stood Mr. Worthington taking off his cap before entering the house, and standing right behind him, with a smirk on his face, was Harlan.

Granny let go of Charley's ear and shaking her fist at him, said, "This Irish devil beggar boy was making fun of an old lady in her own home! Pretending to pull hairs from his chin. I caught him right in the act. He had the girls all wild and hysterical on the floor in a heap. It forebodes bad times! This wicked devil must leave this house before he corrupts your daughters!"

Charley stood there limp and crushed. His hand reached up to rub life back into his crunched ear. He had just tried to make a little fun and it turned out bad. He cussed himself, he should have checked to see if Granny Rozella was around. Now everything was a mess again.

Mr. Worthington looked down at Charley with tired eyes. He sighed, and then said, "I will take care of the young man, Mother. Please leave us alone."

With an indignant, "Humph!" Granny Rozella turned on her heel, clicked her tongue and, holding her head as high as her bent figure would allow her, waddled out of the room.

"Charley, we do not make fun of our elders in this house. You must apologize."

"Sir, I am afraid I cannot do that. She has called me names since the day I came here. Granny Rozella is a mean old witch!" Charley's cheeks flushed red as he brushed past Mr. Worthington and Harlan. His temper was getting the better of him and he knew it. He stomped outside and headed toward the road to town. He thought, I just might be in Boston before my letter to George arrives!

At first the cold night air felt refreshing and it helped to cool Charley's hot temper down. As he strode away from the farm, thoughts of running away rushed through his head. He yearned to see the city lights, feel its energy and smell its sweet and sour scents. He wished he could see Minnie. He hated the way she had disappeared from his life. And why hadn't he heard one word, not one dang word, from Mistress Renée?

Charley was angry, he was angry with all of them! He fought back the stinging tears of disappointment and of . . . what? Of anger . . . of angry hurt that no one wanted him? Maybe he didn't deserve a family. After all, his own parents had left him. He mulled it around in his brain over and over. He couldn't come up with an answer that made any sense. All his anger did was make him fighting mad.

The sun was long gone for the day and the clouds hung dark and heavy. Charley smelled something in the air, damp and cool at the same time. He looked up at the sky and saw snowflakes floating down upon him. The cold wet flakes landed on his face and stuck to his hair. The flurry of light, fluffy flakes soon fell faster, clumping up on his shirt and coveralls. Charley stopped, shaking off the snow. Who was he joking? He wasn't going anywhere, especially all the way to Boston. He had no money for a train ticket and even if he did, how would he get to town? He couldn't just saddle up Chubb and ride him to the station. People would think he stole the horse; besides, he would rather stay way clear of horses.

He had never gotten over his fear of horses since that day when he was helping his pa on the streetcar. He was so proud to be with his pa, Charley wanted to be a part of everything. It was time to feed the horse and his pa was busy attaching the horse's feedbag. Charley had gotten too close to the horse's hoof. The horse spooked and kicked him knocking him down into the curb of the street. His pa saved him from being trampled on.

Charley shivered. In his haste, he hadn't given a thought to a coat or cap. He couldn't go to Boston like this —he would freeze to death. Snow stuck to every part of him. The wind was picking up and the temperature was dropping fast. The first soft flakes of snow had turned to stinging arrows of ice. It was a moonless night and it was getting blacker by the second. He had gone far enough to lose sight of the house, but as he rounded a corner of tall spruce trees, there was the house all lit up and warm-looking inside. It was near suppertime. Charley's stomach did a double rumble. Standing at the door was Laura. He could hear her calling for him, "Chaaaar-leey! Suppertime! Chaaarleey!"

Charley sprinted all the way back to the house.

CHAPTER 15

'Tis the Season to Be Jolly

Charlie had thrown himself into the play, learning his lines until he knew them backwards and forwards. He sang every night after school with the other children who had singing roles. Laura stayed after to watch, even though she had only a small part in the chorus. Charley liked that she stayed so they could walk home together. It was his favorite time of day when the last strands of sunlight captured glistening crystals of snow and the long shadows striped the snowy road home.

He tried not to think about Christmas and how it would be different this year, different from Boston, and different from being at the Home. He tried to concentrate on the play. He wanted it to be his best performance. His singing made him feel good about himself, and he wanted to please Miss Peterson and Mrs. Worthington. He wished he could make Mr. Worthington proud of him. He seemed to be awful hard on him lately. And Harlan was hopeless. How could he ever get along with him? Harlan had had a chip on his shoulder against Charley from the day he came to the farm.

The preparations went on for two weeks before the

play. Every activity centered around it, both at school and at the farm. Charley had been excused from his after-school chores, which meant there was more work for Harlan. Harlan was downright hangdog and nasty looking these days, not having one nice word to say to Charley or anybody for that matter. The most anyone got out of him was a grunt.

The evenings were spent working on the costumes. Mrs. Worthington sewed a red soldier's coat for Charley. She had found an old red woolen blanket that had some moth-eaten holes in it. She cut around the holes and lined it with a shiny fabric that made Charley feel like a real soldier. Laura admired it, telling him that he looked handsome in it. Miss Peterson had loaned him a soldier's fuzzy black hat. And Mr. Worthington was helping him learn how to cut out the shape of a rifle from an old barn board. Laura made him black cuffs to fit around his legs and cover his shoes, so it looked like he had boots on. Granny Rozella's treadle wheel whizzed as she made a furry black cat costume for Lynette.

Laura wanted to play the part of the dog, but Miss Peterson insisted she be the rag doll. She finally agreed to play the part of the doll and sewed yards and yards of underskirts and ruffles on her old dress until it billowed out around her like a bell.

It was, at long last, the day of the play! Every button was sewn in place and each ruffle starched and pressed. At breakfast time, the costumes were laid out on the dining room table.

At the end of the school day Miss Peterson had the children stay for a final practice. Charley sang his lead song better than ever. Excitement was in the air as the chorus sang the last verse of the finale. Miss Peterson told them they all sounded magnificent! Charley, Lynette and Laura raced home, eager to get into their costumes and return early for the warm ups.

"Betcha I'll beat you home, Charley!" Laura's cheeks were pink with excitement.

"Ha, you silly girl, you can't run faster than me!" Charley surged ahead with Laura close on his heels.

Lynette lagged behind and wailed, "Laura Ann, you wait for me! I don't want to walk all by myself!"

Laura slowed her pace for Lynette to catch up, allowing Charley to race home alone. Charley kept running. He didn't mind leaving the girls behind. It felt good to let the cool December air fill his lungs and make his head feel light and free. He was beginning to lose his steam at the final stretch, but with a surge of adrenaline he ran right up to the mudroom and through the kitchen door, letting it bang behind him.

"Why, Charley, you are home early. How did your practice go today?" Mrs. Worthington smiled as she picked the baby up in her arms and bounced it up and down on her lap.

"It went swell! I hope it's as good tonight. I'm just gonna go check on my costume." Charley was gone before Mrs. Worthington could answer. As he whisked around the corner his eyes searched for the bright red coat. He saw the black fur hat and his make believe boots lined up next to his rifle. He saw Laura's dress decorated from top to bottom with ribbons and bows and Lynette's furry kitty costume. But the coat wasn't there. He checked under the table and behind the chairs. No coat!

Charley ran back into the kitchen. "Mrs. Worthington, did you take my jacket? It's not on the dining room table!" Charley tried to calm down, Mrs. Worthington would have a simple explanation.

"Why no, Charley. I didn't move your coat, it was all finished and pressed last night and laid out this morning. It has to be there, no one would have taken it. No one was here all day, except Granny and me. And Harlan, who burst into the kitchen for a piece of bread and jam before he went out to do the farm chores."

"But it's gone!" Charley's cheeks flushed a deep crimson.

"Calm yourself, maybe it was put into your room. Why don't you look for it in there?" Mrs. Worthington placed the baby in her chair within a box and said, "I'll help you look. We shall find it. It must be here somewhere." They walked through the parlor together. Charley noticed that

Granny was missing from her usual place at her sewing machine. They did one more quick inspection of the dining room, but the coat was not there.

"Granny went to lie down, she wasn't feeling well this morning, I am afraid she has a cold. I'll go ask her if she knows where it is, and I will check all the bedrooms while I am upstairs." Mrs. Worthington rubbed her brow. "We shall find it Charley. I'm sure there is some logical explanation behind this mystery." Mrs. Worthington bustled off with her skirts swishing about her as she hurried towards the stairs.

Charley ran to his room, it was just as he had left it. No red jacket! Charley felt uneasy. Could Granny have taken it? She never did like him, although lately they just ignored one another. He made a fist and hit his pillow, he was getting angry.

He stormed out of the house just in time to see Laura and Lynette enter the yard.

"Hey, Laura, do you know where my soldier jacket is? It ain't in the dining room."

"What do ya mean? Your coat was there this morning, all finished and ready for tonight."

"Well it ain't there now, your ma is lookin' upstairs, and it ain't in my room. I don't know where it could be unless," Charley spat out the last three words, *"someone took it!"*

Laura scrunched her face up in thought and then answered, "Let's check the barn."

At that moment Mrs. Worthington stuck her head out the mudroom door. "Charley, I can't find hide nor hair of it! I checked all the bedrooms upstairs, including Harlan's and there is no red coat. Granny was sound asleep. I didn't wake her, but I looked all through her sewing baskets and it is not there. I just don't know what to tell you!"

"We'll find his coat," Laura announced with a sureness that made Charley feel a little hopeful. "Okay, Charley, let's look in the barn!"

"Why would it be in the barn? That don't make no kind of sense to me!" Charley pushed his cap back on his head in exasperation.

"'Cause if it ain't in the house it's gotta be in the barn!"

"You go look in the barn if ya want!" Charley turned his back on Laura and, kicking a stone out of his way, stormed in the direction of the chicken coop. He needed to be alone. He was exasperated. How could this happen? How could he go on stage and sing without his red jacket? He wouldn't look like a soldier. He'd look like a dope. That was the one thing Charley couldn't reckon with, he was too proud to be made a fool of when he sang. Being dumb about farm things frustrated him, but he could sing, and no one could take that away from him, or could they? Then he knew; suddenly, it all made sense. Someone did not want him to sing, someone hid his coat so he couldn't.

Charley heard the chickens clucking inside; they were making more than their usual racket. Curious, he threw open the door to the coop. It slammed with a bang against the rickety building causing the hens to scream with fear. Feathers flew as they scrambled to the farthest corners of the hen house.

Charley looked at the spot where they had been, there on the floor covered with chicken feathers and droppings was his red jacket. Charley winced in disbelief as he bent down to retrieve it. Wide uneven holes marked the spots where the gold buttons once were. The inside fabric was shredded to bits. The pockets were torn and hanging down from the few threads that were not severed away.

Charley felt sick to his stomach. In disbelief, he left the chicken coop. He carried the coat to the pit where the trash was burned. The embers glowed a deep red the same color as his jacket. He dropped the coat on top of the pit. The silken threads of the lining twisted and writhed in the smoke. In a second the entire coat was ablaze.

Laura and Lynette were still in the barn. No one witnessed the burning of the coat but Charley. He pulled his cap on tight and strode back to the house.

"Did you find anything, Charley? No luck in the barn?" Mrs. Worthington's face was etched with concern.

"Nope, no luck." Charley exited the kitchen seeking the safety of his room.

It all hit him like a ton of bricks. He knew what he had to do. He was not welcome in this family and he never could prove himself to be. He simply did not fit in. He wasn't cut out to be a farmer. And Harlan hated him, he was certain of that.

Charley dressed in his best white shirt and his good pants. He shoved his arms into the tweed jacket that he had worn from the Home. It was a little tight, but it would have to do. He went into the dining room and retrieved his black boot leggings that Laura had made him. Then he placed his soldier hat under his arm, and carried his cut out rifle tipped up against his shoulder. He was ready to go. He found himself determined more than ever to sing tonight like he had never sung before. And then after that was done, he would somehow find a way to get back to Boston and find George.

Charley got into position and waited for the lights to dim and the curtains to be pulled open. The seconds ticking by seemed like hours. He saw Laura's silhouette in the shadows, her dress billowing around her making her look twice her size. He knew if he could see her eyes she would encourage him. He didn't need or want Laura tonight. He must do this play on his own. He had to show them he could sing with or without his red jacket.

The curtains were pulled open. Charley stepped forward onto the gas-lit stage. He opened his mouth. The lyrics of the first verse rang out rich and strong, filling the room and more. The audience, enraptured by his voice, sat frozen in their seats. The dog and cat, and all the toys chanted out their chorus lines. But even then, with all their voices joining in, Charley's voice rose above the others, carrying the audience to the highest of heights!

Charley danced with the toys, each one twirling and spinning around the room to a merry foot-tapping tune. The audience swayed in their seats, feeling the rhythm. The dog barked, "Woof, woof, I am the dog." The cat sang out, "Meow, meow, I am the cat." And Laura, the rag doll, came forward to center stage and recited her poem. Then, without warning, long shadows were cast across the stage darkening the joyful scene. In marched the warrior rats! The rats were terrifying with huge teeth and red eyes that glowed. The toys and animals shook with fear. Whimpering, they scurried away to hide behind the shelves and under the bed. Charley, left alone to combat the attack of the rats, struck them down one by one with the butt of his rifle. But the rats fought back. They jumped up from their prone positions to pursue him with their sharp claws trying to capture him at every turn. On a great roll of a drum he raised his rifle and shot them—bang! bang! bang!—leaving them wiggling on the floor until their bodies went stiff.

Charley, triumphant in slaying all the rats, called the toys and animals to come out of hiding. Timidly they peaked out from beneath the bed and behind the shelves. They gathered around Charley and joined in singing the victorious finale.

The applause was deafening. The audience went wild. The curtains were pulled closed but Miss Peterson opened them once more and, beaming with pride, sent Charley back to the stage for another bow. Charley's ears were full of the sound of clapping hands. The whole cast scampered back onto the stage and encircled Charley. They sang the finale as an encore for a second time. The play was a smashing success. The parents committee presented a bouquet of flowers to Miss Peterson. Then the curtains closed for the final time.

"Charley! Ya did real good tonight! I'm so proud of ya!" Laura followed him from behind the stage into the lighted room.

Charley didn't respond to Laura. To his surprise, there, still seated in the last row, was Harlan. Should he confront him right here? Should he demand an apology for ruining his coat? He felt all muddled up inside and confused. Why did Harlan come? Did his parents make him, or did he just want the fun of seeing him flop in the play?

Before he could think any more about what to do about Harlan, furry arms were squeezing him. "Oh! Charley, you sang beautiful! You were the best toy soldier ever!" Lynnette clung to him, acting more like a black furry monkey than a cat.

Other folks were clapping him on the back and telling him, "Good job there, Charley, you sure can carry a tune!" and, "Boy, oh boy, Charley, you sure can sing!"

With tears in her eyes, Mrs. Worthington approached him, throwing her arms around his neck. "My dear Charley! I'm so proud of you! You sang like an angel!"

"Thank you, ma'am." Charley, flushed and overwhelmed with the attention, suddenly wanted the night to be over and done with. The crowd was dispersing and Charley noticed that Harlan had left the room along with Mr. Worthington. There would be no confrontation tonight. It was time to head back to the farm.

Tired and happy families climbed into their wagons and snuggled together as they headed home on this crisp evening. The children, tucked under layers of woolen blankets, were dreaming of making spicy gingerbread men to hang on their Christmas trees. Soon it would be Christmas day.

⋆⇒ ⇐⋆

Laura stuck her head into Charley's room. "Charley! Wake up! It's Christmas morning!"

Charley groaned, "I don't care about Christmas! Go away!"

"Oh, Charley, come on, get up! Don't you want to open your presents?"

"Presents for me? You're kidding?"

"Ha, you will just have to come see for yourself! Come on, hurry!"

Charley threw his robe on and walked out into the dark kitchen. He wondered what time it was. He hadn't heard the rooster crow. He made his way into the parlor. On top of the table sat a little evergreen tree. They had decorated it last night with cut out paper ornaments and gingerbread cookies. It smelled spicy, of cinnamon and ginger. Laura had lit the kerosene lamp and was rummaging through all the presents. She was busy sorting them into piles.

"Laura, what are you doing? It's the middle of the night!"

"No it ain't! It's almost four in the morning, and I couldn't wait one more minute. Look here, this is your pile. Open this one first, it's from your sister Minnie!" Laura handed him a box wrapped in brown paper and tied with a string. Before he could begin to untie the string Laura said, "Oh, Charley, this is a letter from the Home. Do ya think it could be from your singing teacher? The one that was your mistress?"

Laura was going way too fast for Charley. Everything was swimming before his eyes. There was a present from Minnie? He had never seen it arrive. He had to open it first. He untied the string and then unpeeled the wrapping paper. He held the rectangular box in his hands. It had printing on the top. The script was so fancy it was hard to read. He opened the hinged box to uncover its mysterious contents. It was silver and it shone bright in the light of the lamp. He brought it up to his lips and felt the cool metal and wood against them. He puffed air into it. It made a soft note. He puffed again and then again, going up and down the scales. All the while, his heart hurt from missing Minnie's pretty face smiling up at him. Why couldn't she be here with him, to see him open his present? He would have played a tune just for her.

"Oh, Charley! What did she send you? It plays music!" Laura reached her hand out to touch it. Charley allowed her to examine it. "What does it say on the top, Charley, it has such fancy letters?"

At her request Charley read the inscription aloud, "Boston Music Company, Newbury Street, Boston." Charley felt choked up. He not only missed Minnie, he missed Boston, too. He slipped the harmonica into the pocket of his robe. He would play it later when he was alone.

Charley, filled with curiosity, picked up the envelope that was sent from the Home. He recognized the delicate strokes of Mistress Renée's handwriting. His hands shook with anticipation as he tore open the flap of the envelope. Inside was a Christmas card with a glittery picture of couples skating arm in arm on the Boston Common. He flipped the card over to see what she had written:

Charley, mon ami,
> *I am coming to Greene, Maine, with my choir, the third Sunday in January. I wish for you to sing with us! We will sing all the same songs that you know so well.*
> *Wishing you a Joyous Noel!*
> *Mistress Renée*

Charley should have been thrilled at the prospect of seeing Mistress Renée. He should be jumping for joy. Part of him wanted her to come so he could return with her to Boston and Minnie and George. They would send for Clarence and be a family again. But on the other hand, he couldn't fool himself any longer. It was stupid to keep hoping for this reunion. And besides, part of him was angry with Mistress Renée and the Home; they had both failed him. Had Mistress Renée or anyone else come from the Home to check on whether he was happy or not? Like she had promised? How could he trust her, or the Home?

"Hey, Charley, here, open my present! I made it myself!" Laura held a soft package all covered in hand-colored paper and tied with a bright red ribbon. Charley slipped the card into its envelope and dropped it into his robe pocket next to the harmonica. "C'mon, Charley, you are so slow, open it! You're going to be surprised!"

Charley accepted Laura's offering of her present and held it in his hands before opening it. He felt numb inside. Laura stared at him intently, watching his every move. He pulled the end of the ribbon, freeing the package so the paper came away easily. "Merry Christmas, Charley! I made it myself, well, Mom helped me a little." Laura's eyes glistened. "I couldn't sleep all night, waiting for morning to give you my present!"

Charley pulled the knotted yarn away from the wrapping and held it up in the air to determine what it was. One end was twice the size of the other, giving it a triangular shape. He was pretty certain it was a scarf, but he had never seen one quite like this before. "It's a scarf, Charley; try it on!"

Charley, responding to Laura's plea, wrapped it around his neck. The tail hung down to his knees. The scarf was wooly and scratchy on his bare neck. His hand gravitated to his robe pocket. The rectangular box that contained the silver harmonica from Minnie was still there, and beside it the glittery card from Mistress Renée with the announcement of her return to Greene, Maine. Charley felt deeply confused, all his emotions were fighting with each other and he felt beat up by them. Sadness fell over him like a curtain closing against the sun. Could he trust Mistress Renée? Would he ever get back to Boston? Would the Home take him back? Did they even care about him? Would he be able to make it on his own? He was floundering in his thoughts when Laura tugged on the sleeve of his robe. She peered at him expectantly.

"Laura, I got to go back to my room." Charley's head was swimming. He hadn't given a thought about a present for Laura. "I um, I um . . . I got something for you back in my room." Laura watched him walk away from her with the scarf still wrapped around his neck. He opened the door to his room and went straight for his box. He knew what he should do. He would give her his shooter marble. She would like that. He didn't have time to wrap it, or anything to wrap it with, for that matter. He had to hurry and give it to her before Granny Rozella woke up!

CHAPTER 16

Cutting Ice

S leigh bells rang out in the crisp January air. Snow crunched beneath Chubb and Maude's heavy hooves as they pulled the sleigh wagon through the woods to the snowy banks of the town pond. The wagon coasted to a slow stop. Laura was the first to jump out of the wagon, with Charley quick to follow. He had never seen such a sight in his life. Horse-drawn sleighs and wagons peppered the edge of the frozen pond. Small bonfires were lit, crackling with golden flames to warm frozen fingers and toes. Whole families were at work clearing off large patches of snow to expose the thick layer of ice below. Children charged down piles of snow, throwing snowballs and slip-sliding on cleared pathways of ice. Peals of laughter resounded in the air from the youngest children, while the older ones joined in to help the grownups with the all-important task at hand, the ice harvest.

Mr. Worthington nodded to several of the other men as he made his way to a section of ice that was not yet claimed in the middle of the pond. Charley helped to carry some of the tools they would use that day to cut the ice. They were all new to him; he had seen them hanging in the barn, but he had never known what they were used for. Laura came along carrying a pair of tongs almost as big as

her. Charley dragged a slew of shovels behind him while
Harlan slung what he called the ice chisel and breaker bar
over his shoulder. Mr. Worthington carried the rest. As
they arrived at their destination each took a shovel and set
to work clearing the snow from the ice.

A girl, from the neighboring Anderson family, ran to
greet Laura. Her cheeks were flushed pink with the cold.
"May Laura and Lynette come sliding with me? My papa
made us a slide clear away from the cutting holes. He says
it is good and safe." Mr. Worthington nodded his approval,
and Laura and Lynette ran off eager for a good slide.

Charley wished he could slide too, but instead he continued to clear the snow from the ice. It was heavy work,
for it had already snowed many times this year. The layers
of snow made him think about the first snow and how he
had gone back to the house that night, the night he had to
apologize to Granny. It burned inside him to have to say
he was sorry. The crabby old witch had just sniffed and
turned away, but Mr. Worthington forgave him and that
was all he needed. Granny Rozella was just crazy and there
was nothing he could do about that.

"Okay, boys, I'm ready to start making the lines for our
cuts. Charley, this here tool with the long serrated edge is
called the hand plow. It cuts into the top layer of the ice to
make a nice straight line. When all the lines are cut it will
look like one big checkerboard." Mr. Worthington used the
hand plow and etched the ice into even squares. "I want
you to follow along the lines when you cut the ice, that
way we will get nice square blocks. Harlan, you start the

first block. Charley, you watch Harlan. Once you get the hang of it you and Harlan will be takin' turns."

Harlan picked up one of the breaker bars and chopped straight down into the farthest corner of the ice. Soon he had a hole deep enough to insert the saw into. Charley watched the blade disappear into the ice. Harlan held the wooden handles on the top of the saw and slid the blade up and down at a perfect forty-five degree angle. He made it look as easy as if he were slicing a piece of cake. He cut through the second side of the cube and then down the third. Now he was ready for the last cut. He put the saw down and took a two-pronged breaker bar. He chopped straight into the line on the ice. After several tries Charley heard a thud. One more chop and the cube floated free.

"That thudding sound is the ice breaking away. Get the tongs and pull her out!" Harland ordered.

Charley grabbed the tongs and was surprised at their heft. He tried to stick the tongs into the slits on either side of the cube, but when he pulled they just slipped right off. Mr. Worthington sighed as he watched Charley struggling. He took the tongs from Charley and proceeded to slide the ice cube out of the water and over the edge to lie flat on the frozen ice. "First one is the hardest, they get easier as you go 'cause they break loose in the water. This one here is especially tight. Harlan, cut her nice and even."

Once the cube was out of the water, Charley picked up the saw and started to cut the line to form the second cube. The ice fought him and the blade wobbled in its track. Charley placed his feet firmly on the ice outside the cutting area. He pulled the blade up and then pushed it back down again. He could feel the steam escaping from inside his coat, out his neck and arms. Up and down, up and down. He figured he must be close enough to the end. The blade was well past the top of the line. He thought it might speed things up if he gave the saw a good solid wiggle. Harlan yipped, "Don't wiggle it, you'll break the blade. Just keep it straight! If you're too tired, I can take over."

"No! Harlan, give me a chance, I can do it!" Charley snapped back. Boy, Harlan sure could get his goat. Charley forged on, managing to cut two sides. Harlan used the breaker bar and had the cube free in a second. Charley grabbed it with the tongs and tipped it out onto the ice. It was Harlan's turn to do the sawing. Harlan with his long arms made faster and deeper cuts than Charley's.

Now it was Charley's turn to try the breaker bar. He found it frustrating. He used all his strength to chop into the ice as deep as he could. He listened hard, but no thudding sound reached his ears. He needed to take a breather. He could hear Laura laughing as she ran across the ice with the Anderson girl, taking long slides. A twinge of envy crept over him. He wished he could be sliding on the ice with Laura, not cutting it with a stupid breaker bar.

Harlan hauled the ice cube he had cut to the wagon. Mr. Worthington set the cube in the wagon. It went on and on, Charley cutting, Harlan chipping, the tongs pulling the ice out and then the harvested cube being hauled to the wagon and stacked. They had twelve cubes cut. It was Charley's turn once again to use the breaker bar. His

arms were aching and his fingers were raw on the inside of his woolen mittens. Chip, chip, chip went the breaker bar. No sound of a thud. Sweat was pouring down his face. He opened the top button on his jacket to let some steam out.

"C'mon, Charley, hurry up and cut off this cube so we can eat lunch. Ma packed us chicken stew with biscuits!" Harlan sounded friendly or at least hungry.

"I can't seem to break this here one free." Charley pushed his cap to the back of his head and wiped the sweat off of his face with a wet woolen mitten.

"Well, sometimes ya get a stinker. You just give her a good stomp and off she comes." Harlan turned to retrieve the tongs that had slid a short distance from the open hole of water.

With every bit of strength he had left, Charley stomped the ice cube with the heel of his right boot. It didn't budge. In utter frustration, Charley jumped with both feet onto the cube. He heard a dull thud.

Whoosh! The world tilted crazily.

The next thing he knew he was under water. Freezing, brain-numbing, frigid water engulfed every part of him. His woolen coat and layers of clothing soaked up the water like a hungry sponge. His boots were lead weights pulling him down deeper as the water seeped into his double layers of heavy socks. He was terrified! Would he drown in this frozen hole? He forced his eyes open. The water stung, sending a shooting pain through his skull. He focused on a patch of light directly above him. With a rush of adrenaline he made a super human effort to surge to the top of the open hole. He felt the cold fresh air. The clear blue sky flashed open above him. He heard someone screaming his name.

He greedily sucked in the fresh air as he reached upwards to grab a hold of something, anything, that might keep him from going back under. His soaking mittens sought desperately to grasp the edge of the thick ice. A hand was stretched out towards him. Then something hard collided with the back of his head. Stars flashed across a night sky. The ink black hole of freezing water claimed him once again.

⊷⇒ CHAPTER 17 ⇐⊷

Fever

Someone was moaning, he could hear it low and sad. He wondered "Who could it be?" There it came again, the moan. With all his might he tried to open his eyes, but the light in the room blinded him. Then, it came again. This time it sounded closer, almost on top of him. He struggled to open his eyes just a sliver. His vision blurred and his eyes stung. He blinked them closed, then tried again. He felt water in them; cold, cold water. He wished he could sink back into the safety of deep sleep. But the moan came again. Bewildered, he wondered where he was. He tried opening one eye. The room was hazy and still. Someone was breathing; he could hear it soft and slow. He forced both eyes open, then blinked them closed in pain. Who was sitting next to him? Why was she staring at him?

"Ma! I think he's waking up! Ma! Come quick! I saw his eyes move and he's moanin'!"

The spoken words came out sharp and quick, piercing into the fog surrounding his brain. What did they mean? Who was that girl? Where was he? He couldn't remember.

"Charley! Charley! Wake up! You've been asleep for three whole days. Ya had a bad fever. I bet it's broken now. Charley! Boy, oh boy, you talked like the dickens. Mostly, I couldn't understand a durn thing you was talking about.

Exceptin' when you was asking for your mama, that part I understood." Charley forced his eyes to open. He stared at her for a moment then his eyes clamped shut. Who was that girl?

A plump, friendly-looking woman rushed into the room, wiping her hands on a towel. She placed the palm of her hand, which was warm and slightly moist, on Charley's forehead. "Yes, yes, I do believe his fever has broke, thank the Lord. Now we must get some hot soup into him. Laura, honey, get him to drink so he doesn't get dehydrated. I'll fetch some soup from the pot in the hearth."

Charley's head hurt and there was a dull buzzing in his ears. His eyes were slowly adjusting to the filtered light in the room. *Laura, she called the girl Laura!* He knew that name from somewhere. He struggled to remember. Why was he in this bed? Why did he hurt all over his body? He tried to move under the layers of covers. He groaned out loud. The girl was cradling his head with her hand, trying to lift it up. He wanted to help her, but he couldn't. Everything hurt, especially his lungs. He felt like they had been turned inside out. He tried to focus his eyes on her, the girl, the one named Laura. She was smiling at him. She held the cup up to his mouth and he felt the cool water touch his lips. "Come on, Charley, ya gotta drink this! We gotta get ya better."

Charley did his best to take in the water. His throat was raw and sore. The cool water felt good in his mouth and against his tongue, but it was so painful to swallow that most of it dribbled down his chin. He raised his hand to wipe it away. When he saw his hand he sucked in his breath. It was wrapped in a gauze bandage.

"Oh, Charley, I am so sorry; how clumsy of me! Let me wipe it up." She put his head back down on the pillow gingerly and reached for a towel. He examined her face as she dabbed his chin and neck. His eyes were fully open now. He needed to concentrate, to focus his thoughts.

"Where am I?" Charley croaked.

"Why, Charley, you're in your room. You've been sleeping since we brought you home. You nearly froze to death! Don't cha remember? You fell in the ice pond; you were cutting ice, and you fell right in!" The girl Laura's face was animated, appearing eager to tell him the rest of the story.

"I didn't see you fall in, but when Harlan yelled for Pa, I heard him and came running. Your head was below the water and I was so afraid you'd get lost under the ice, but you popped right back up. Did ya hear me screaming your name? Pa stretched himself flat on the ice and reached his hand out to grab you. Harlan had the big tongs to help pull ya out, like an ice cube, but he moved too quick and chinked ya in the back of the head then ya slid back under. Charley it was awful!"

It was starting to come back, something cold all around him, freezing cold and then the blackness. "How did I get out?" Charley's voice was raspy. It hurt to talk.

"Well, you was under for a while, seemed like forever. I was crying and begging for you to be saved. Pa stuck his arm into the water as deep as he could without fallin' in himself, and Harlan waited with the tongs. Then we saw you, 'cause you floated up to the top again. Harlan did it right this time and grabbed your whole self with the tongs. He said you were heavier than anything and you was half froze ta death. Pa and some other men helped pull you out and laid you down on the ice. He pushed your stomach and made ya throw up all the water ya took in."

"I threw up?"

"Ya, you did! But everybody was happy 'cause that meant ya didn't drown and your insides was workin'. But your outsides was frozen bad. Pa carried ya over to the bonfire but it wasn't warm enough 'cause your coat and everythin' was frozen right on ya. Pa had to cut the buttons off your coat to get it off ya. Then, when he got everything cut off, he wrapped ya up like a baby in a blanket. Well, a lot of blankets really."

"He cut my clothes off?" Charley had no recollection of any of this, but where he was now was beginning to come back to him. He had come from Boston to live on a farm, a farm in Maine. And this girl, Laura, lived on the farm.

"We had to hurry to return you back home, to get you warm. But you never woke up! The doctor rode out here in his horse and buggy. He said your heart was good but that you had a sky-high fever. He said you'd get a bad case of pneumonia 'cause your lungs got frozen. Do ya? Do ya think you got a bad case?"

"I don't know, but my lungs hurt like the devil. Boy, I sure am hungry." Charley gave Laura a flicker of a smile.

"Here comes the soup!" Mrs. Worthington announced as she reentered the room. "But we must take it slow since you have not eaten in three days. Your poor stomach will not know what to do with it." She shooed Laura aside. "You go watch the baby now; I will take care of Charley."

She raised a half-filled spoon up to Charley's lips. The soup tasted good and hot going down his sore throat. His desire to eat overcame his pain. He slurped down as much as Mrs. Worthington would allow him. Then, exhausted, he closed his eyes and fell asleep.

The room was dark when Charley woke. He closed his eyes and listened to the muffled sounds coming from the kitchen. Must be suppertime, he thought. His stomach growled like a bear waking up from hibernation. He'd had a taste of the soup and now he wanted more. The warmth of the kitchen stove filled his room and the smells of home-made bread filled his nostrils.

He wondered why his hands were bandaged. He wiggled his fingers to find out if they still worked. They did. He wiggled his toes and they worked too. If only he didn't have a raging headache and the horrible pain in his chest. He tried to rearrange himself to sit up, but he was most comfortable flat on his back. He could hear Laura babbling on and on. That girl sure could talk. He wondered what he had said when he was sleeping. Did he really ask for his mother? He felt like an idiot! And all that Laura had relayed to him about what happened was durn right humiliating.

Now there were only two voices in the kitchen speaking low and serious. He strained to hear their words. "I am sorry, Mary. It just isn't working to keep the boy. He is not cut out for farm work. We lost a good milking Holstein cow because of him and now we didn't get our fair share of the ice cutting done. When Harlan and I went back, there were only some scrappy pieces of ice left. They won't last us through the summer. I'll have to beg some off of Jake Anderson, then we will be obliged to him."

Charley's ears burned hot. What had been a dull buzz in his head now hissed like a nest of angry hornets.

"But Edwin, the boy needs to be nourished back to health. The doctor said it takes a long time to cure a bad case of pneumonia, sometimes months."

"That's just what I mean, Mary. He'll be sickly now for most of the winter, taking up your time to nurse him. I think we should send the boy back as soon as he is able to ride the train to Boston."

Charley wanted to cover his ears, but both hands were bandaged and sore. When was Mistress Renée coming? It should be soon, he had lost count of days and time. Was it the third weekend? How many weeks had gone by? "When she comes," he thought, "I'll leave this farm, forever!"

⤙⤙ CHAPTER 18 ⤚⤚

The Surprise Visit

"Hey, Charley, ya got a visitor!" Laura popped her head into his room, grinning with delight. "Your Mistress is here! Boy, oh boy! She sure is pretty!"

Charley lay there helpless. He didn't want her to see him, not like this. He felt a failure and a fool. He wasn't ready for her to come. His hands were still bandaged from the frostbite, and his lungs felt raspy and sore.

"No, Laura. I can't see her now. She's supposed to come the third Sunday in January. Not today!" Charley wanted to curl up into a ball and hide. He didn't want her to see him at his worst.

"Charley, she's in the parlor with Ma right now. I can't send her away. I thought this would make you happy!" Laura frowned at him. "Anyways, today is Sunday, Charley! The third Sunday in January!"

"Today is the third Sunday of January? The choir from the Home must be singing today. Shoot! I was supposed to sing with them." Charley blinked back dry tears.

"*Bonjour, mon ami! Bonjour*, Charley!" Mistress Renée's voice floated into the room. Charley was afraid to look at her. He had a lump in his throat the size of a baked potato. His chest felt as heavy as if someone were sitting on it, pinning him down.

Charley could hear her soft steps as she walked across the room to his bedside. She touched him lightly on the shoulder. He could smell her perfume, like fresh flowers. Tears of embarrassment splashed down his burning cheeks as he turned his gaze away from her.

"Oh, my sweet Charley, please do not feel bad because I am here! I did not know of your accident until I reached the church and I asked for you to sing with us. The pastor told me this most terrible story about you coming so close to freezing to death underneath the ice. I came as soon as I could." Charley turned towards her. Mistress Renée was as beautiful as ever.

"Now, Charley, you must work hard to get better. Mrs. Worthington has assured me that you will be in her good care. She is such a lovely lady and she cares very much about you!"

He had to ask, "Why? Why didn't you come to see me? No one from the Home ever came. You said someone would come." He felt stupid, like he was a baby blubbering.

"Oh my Charley, I could not come with my choir until now. It is a very long way to travel. And, *mon ami*, your brother George came to the Home and told Reverend Matthews and myself that you were doing very well. He said that you had a friend named Laura, and you were learning how to be a farmer. Reverend Mathews didn't feel it was necessary to send someone so far if you were doing fine."

Charley wanted to scream! How could George have told the reverend that he was fine when he wasn't? Charley wanted to spill out his guts and tell her everything. Everything that had happened since the day he came to the farm. He wanted to tell her about the cow dying, about Harlan and the red coat ruined, and about Granny Rozella calling him names and snatching away his shooter marble. But he knew that Laura was leaning against the wall near the door. He couldn't speak of any of this, not in front of Laura.

Instead he croaked, "But, I wanted to sing . . . to sing with the choir!"

"Oh, Charley! *Oui!* You will sing again! I want you to get all of your strength back and then you can maybe come to visit me at the Home. You will sing with the choir! I will send you two tickets so you can come and bring your sweet friend Laura. Now, *excusez moi,* I must go! The children are waiting for me at the church, and we have to catch the train for the long ride back to Boston. *Au revoir,* my Charley." She kissed his forehead and then turned vanishing from the room. Charley breathed in the air that smelled of her and closed his eyes. Her face lit up the inside of his eyelids. At first, he hadn't wished to see her, but now he didn't want her to go, not without him.

"Hey, Charley, wanna play checkers?" Laura's slight figure slipped into the space where Mistress Renée had just been. "That'll cheer ya up. I'll even let cha win!"

"How can a guy play checkers with his hands wrapped up like sausages?" Charley really wished she would go away, so he could think about Mistress Renée.

"I'll go ask Ma if we can cut them bandages off. They've been on long enough. I heard the doc saying them bandages was only needed for a couple of days. They're meant to keep the skin from peeling off 'cause of your frostbite. He said chances are ya wouldn't lose any of 'em, I mean your fingers. It's just 'cause they got wet when your mittens fell off. Then they got froze and that sometimes makes the skin come off. You can get yourself a durn awful infection."

"Maybe we better leave 'em on and just not play checkers!" Charley didn't have the stomach right now to see what his hands looked like.

"Naw, I'll get Ma and some scissors." Laura skipped out of the room returning with her mother.

"Charley, this is a big day for you! A visit from your sweet teacher, she was so concerned for you. Now, just hold your hand still and I will have this bandage off of you in no time at all." Mrs. Worthington set to work and Charley watched as the layers fell away. His fingers didn't hurt so much anymore, and he could move them around inside the bandages, but he was nervous to see them. He closed one eye and peered down nervously with the other. The last wrapping came undone. Stunned, Charley stared at his hand. Patches of skin had fallen off leaving red, raw spots. The skin that remained looked like scabs of brittle leather. Charley recoiled within himself, he felt ugly, as if he were a leper.

"Oh my, your hands are worse than what I thought. Well, let's get some air on them. Tonight I'll grease and wrap them back up for you. The grease helps the scabs come off without leaving scars." Mrs. Worthington set to work unwrapping the bandages on his other hand.

Lynette stuck her head in the room, "Hey! What cha doin' to Charley?"

"Just cutting off his bandages. Go away!" Laura snapped at her sister.

"All of you go away!" Charley felt his blood boil, his patience long gone. "Go away! Go away and leave me alone!"

⋆⇥◯ ◯⇤⋆

Charley was sitting at the kitchen table hunched over his paper work for school. "Charley, you got a letter! I bet it's from your brother, George!" Laura and Lynnette brought in a sudden blast of frigid air as they marched through the mudroom into the warmth of the kitchen. Laura deposited the letter in front of Charley's nose and then, pulling off her mittens, said, "Pa went to town today and he gave us a ride home from school. He gave me the letter to give to you!"

Just then the door banged open, once more filling the room with a blast of chilly air. Harlan sauntered up to the table. Snatching up the letter, he mockingly fanned himself with it. "Wonder what your big brother has to say? Maybe he wants you to go back to Boston and work in the factory like him?" Harlan threw the letter down onto the table and, not waiting for an answer, sauntered out of the kitchen and through the mudroom door.

"Don't you pay no mind to mean old Harlan. He's just steamin' 'cause he has to do all your chores. But you're getting better all the time now, Charley, aren't cha? Why, you'll be coming back to school soon, won't cha?" Laura ripped her coat and hat off, hanging them on a chair near the stove. She slid into the chair next to Charley and blinked her big brown eyes at him. "C'mon, Charley, let's read your letter!"

Charley, still angry with George for lying to Reverend Matthews, tore the back flap of the envelope and opened the letter. His eyes scanned the page for any good news. One word jumped right off of the page. He stared, stunned, at the letters scribbled by George. It couldn't be true. It must be a mistake. He read it out loud as if he didn't understand what the word meant: "Deceased?"

"Who's diseased?" Laura questioned. Lynnette stood behind Laura's chair, looking at Charley with worried eyes.

"Deceased. That means dead. Someone stamped 'deceased' across George's letter, the last one he wrote to my dad." Charley's stomach hurt like someone kicked him with a hobnailed boot. He shook his head in disbelief, then with letter in hand he walked in a daze out of the kitchen into the solitude of his own room. His head was swimming as he forced himself to sit down on the edge of his bed and read the letter from beginning to end. Maybe, then, he could make some kind of sense out of it.

Dear Charley,

I'm afraid I got bad news for you. The last letter I sent to Dad came back. They stamped "Deceased" on the envelope. All the letters I sent him came back. I am sorry to have to tell you this but it means Dad's not coming back.

Minnie is happy at the Taylors. They told the Home they want to adopt Minnie. They are sending her to a good school and buy her everything she needs. I went to visit her last weekend and she had a pretty bonnet on and she was smiling until I told her about Pa, then she cried. But I think it will be all for the best that she is adopted by good people. See, before they couldn't adopt her cause of Dad still being alive, but now they can.

Clarence isn't happy with the place he was sent to, he says they work him too hard. He told me he was gonna' run away. I told him to stay put. I will go to New England Home and talk with the Reverend and see what he can do for him.

I heard you fell in the ice pond. Mistress Renée took Minnie out to tea to talk about being adopted and she told her all about it. I hope you are feeling better. Charley, you are lucky you have a family that is willing to take care of you. Don't go telling me you want

to come back to Boston. It is freezing here, the factory
is cold and damp all day long and then I come home to
a flat with no real heat, just an old pipe that whines
and spits hot water at ya!
     Your brother,
     George

Charley crumpled up the letter and threw it across the
room. He was angry, fighting angry! He would never see
his father ever again. He'd like to shake him hard and
scream at him, right in his face! Why did he have to leave
them? Charley's head was spinning and he had a funny
metallic taste in his mouth. He wasn't sure if he was going
to throw up or burst into tears like a baby. He threw himself across his bed grabbing onto his pillow and stuffing his
face hard into it, hoping to stifle the wracking sobs that
were mounting up inside of him.

Charley felt someone gently touch his shoulder. He
shrugged sharply away from the offending hand. He refused
to pull his face from the pillow. He didn't have the desire
to talk to anyone, not even Laura.

"Charley, are you okay? Are ya upset about your Pa
being stamped 'deceased' on George's letters? Can I read
the letter? It's over there all crumpled up on the floor."

"Go away, Laura. I don't want to talk to anyone."

Laura whispered in Charley's ear, "But, Charley, you
can tell me, I'm your best friend."

Charley sat bolt upright, letting the pillow fall away
from his face. Charley's eyes narrowed as he glared at her,

his face muscles frozen in anger. Laura took a step away from him, stuttering, "Why, I'm sorry Charley, I guess you want to be left alone."

"Go away! Leave me alone. Everybody can just leave me alone. I can take care of myself. I don't need you or your stupid family! As soon as Mistress Renée sends me a ticket to Boston I'm out of here and I ain't comin' back! I hate this stinkin' farm."

⊷⊨⊐ CHAPTER 19 ⊨⊐⊷

Train Tickets

M ud! The ruts in the road from the wagon wheels were two to three feet deep. The melting snow caused it. The snow melted and the frozen earth melted, creating a thick chocolate-colored mud. Laura told Charley the only good thing about the mud was that it meant spring was near.

Charley was back to his chores before school, picking the eggs and feeding the hogs. He carried the wood in for the stove and cleaned out the stalls once the cows were milked and put out to pasture. He was happy to be back at school. It was getting pretty boring being at home all day with only crabby old Granny Rozella, Mrs. Worthington and the baby.

By the time Charley got home from school he was tired. He still did not have the strength he used to have. It was taking him much longer to recover from the pneumonia than he thought it would take, that's what the doc must have meant by a bad case.

Charley waited impatiently for his letter from Mistress Renée with the train tickets to Boston. He sure hoped she didn't forget about sending them. He wouldn't take Laura with him, because then he would be stuck with returning her. She was being a little cool to him lately, since he got the letter from George and blew up at her. Charley tried to be nice to her but she was a girl after all and she had feelings; he must have bruised them a little. He usually walked back and forth to school with her and Lynette, but yesterday Harlan had shown up to walk home with them, and that made Charley feel like the odd man out. Today he had stayed after school to finish some of his missed work. The Worthingtons left without him, so he walked by himself. The good part about that was that it gave him some time to think, and he needed to do some real hard thinking.

He remembered that after his accident, when he had a burning fever, Mr. Worthington said he wanted to send him back once he was well enough to ride the train. He wondered if Mr. Worthington had forgotten about it or if he really meant it. He certainly never talked to Charley about it. Did he write a letter to Reverend Matthews and not tell him? Did Mrs. Worthington talk him out of sending him back? Or maybe Mr. Worthington was simply waiting till mud season was over. The roads were not passable most of the way to town. Charley had seen with his own eyes how they had to scrape the mud off of the roads and lay down planks of wood to keep the wheels of the wagons from sinking. Oh heck, he told himself, it didn't matter if it was the mud or not, or if Mr. Worthington wrote a letter or not—he was going to Boston as soon as he got the ticket!

Charley reached the house. He was tired and Mrs. Worthington would have a cup of hot tea with honey in it for him and some homemade cookies. Heavenly smells of brown sugar, ginger, and spice filled Charley's nose as he opened the back door. To Charley's surprise the kitchen was empty. Charley plopped down his bag of books and lunch pail on the table. There sitting on the table was a letter addressed to him. It had the delicate handwriting he knew so well. He ripped it open and as he unfolded the letter two tickets fell out onto the checkered tablecloth. Charley's hands were shaking with excitement as he scooped them up. He held them close to himself, hugging them. Yes, this was it, what she had promised: two round-trip tickets from Greene, Maine, to Boston. Charley held the tickets up in the air, reading the times and dates printed on them, but suddenly his heart stopped, the date was wrong! It said February 26th return trip February 28th. The dates were for last weekend. Just today Miss Peterson had flipped the calendar to the month of March.

"Hey, Charley, whatcha got?" Laura snuck around the corner so quickly Charley didn't see her coming. He slipped the tickets back into the folds of the letter and tucked it deep into the envelope.

"I saw the letter on the table when I came home. Ma said that Mr. Anderson made the trip to town today on horseback so he picked up our mail. I guess it has been sitting in the box for a long while. So what's in it? You put something in it, like tickets, didn't cha?" Laura had that stubborn, inquisitive look that by now Charley knew was trouble.

"Oh, it was just a letter from Minnie, she sent me tickets to her school play. It's already over so I missed it anyways." Charley felt stupid, he wasn't a good liar. But he couldn't let Laura know that they were train tickets to Boston and one of them was meant for her, even if it was too late. He hoped that he could trade one in.

"Too bad you missed Minnie's play." Laura tilted her head to one side and gave him a cold disbelieving look.

⋯⊨⊜ ⊜⊨⋯

"Laura Ann, I don't know what has gotten into you! You are moping around the house all the time and you have been crabby with your sisters, even little baby Lana can do nothing right. Is something bothering you?" Mrs. Worthington spoke just loud enough for Charley to hear. His ears pricked up as he entered the mudroom.

"Nothing's bothering me! And I'm not moping!" Laura put her hands on her hips and stuck out her chin as far as her neck would go.

Charley stifled a chuckle. Laura sure was a funny girl. Then his mind jumped ahead to guess what they might be talking about. Oh no, he thought, I hope she doesn't tell her mother what I said. Maybe I should let them know I'm here. Laura won't say anything in front of me. But he stayed silent hidden in the mudroom, listening to what Mrs. Worthington had to say.

"I know my Laura well enough, and I know when something or someone is troubling her. So don't try to hide it from me. You might as well spill the beans. You will feel better about whatever it is if you do."

"Who spilled the beans?" Lynette piped up as she entered the kitchen from the dining room.

"You mind your own p's and q's, Lynette, or I'll flip you into the hog bin." Laura scrunched her face up, mean-like, crossing her eyes at Lynette.

"That is exactly what I am talking about! You are being nasty to everyone and especially your sister. Now that is just about enough of that kind of rude behavior." Mrs. Worthington sounded exasperated; then she sighed and, putting her arms around both Laura and Lynette, gave them a motherly embrace.

"Now that you both are here, I wanted to tell you that as soon as the roads are passable, we are all going on a family outing to town. We have been cooped up all winter, and we all need some new things at the general store. I have our egg and butter money saved up, so you will each be able to purchase a special treat."

"Will Charley come too?" Lynette asked.

"Why, he most certainly may. He is all better now, just gets a little tired now and then." Mrs. Worthington smiled warmly at her daughters.

"He won't come! I betcha anything, he won't come! He doesn't like us anymore!" Laura's voice ratcheted several notches up, finally cracking. She stomped out of the kitchen, leaving Mrs. Worthington and Lynette with bewildered looks on their faces. Charley, unnoticed, slipped out the mudroom door into the chill of the early March afternoon.

⁖⇨ CHAPTER 20 ⇦⁖

Smoke Signals

"But, Charley, why won't you come to town with us? Don't you like us anymore?" Lynette whined. She sat wedged in the back of the wagon next to her sister. Laura held her head rigidly forward, refusing to look in Charley's direction. Mr. Worthington, in the driver's seat, held onto the reins with both hands, keeping the horses still with Harlan silent at his side. Mrs. Worthington and baby Lana settled into the back of the wagon next to the girls.

"I got some things I gotta do, and besides I promised I'd finish up painting the chicken coop." Charley pushed his cap back on his head and waved goodbye as Mr. Worthington tugged the reins and told Maude and Chubb to git. The horses whinnied and, shaking their long manes, pranced forward forcing the wheels of the wagon into motion. Charley sighed. He'd spent nearly three quarters of a whole year with this family, and today was the day he would leave them.

He gathered up the paint pot and well-worn brushes and set to whitewashing the chicken coop. He thought about how much time he had spent in that coop chasing those silly chickens around. He knew the old egg-laying hens by name. He had tamed them with his lullabies, and sassy Bertha didn't even peck at him anymore. He sure enough enjoyed his breakfasts of their fresh fried eggs and hash brown potatoes topped with a hunk of pork rind.

Charley finished the last strokes and admired his work. At least he was not leaving a job unfinished. He cleaned the brushes at the pump and washed out what little paint was left in the bucket. He put them where he found them, in the shed next to the barn. Now it was time to pack up his things. He entered through the mudroom door into the kitchen. The house was quiet and it felt cold without Mrs. Worthington in the kitchen cooking. He went straight to his room and opened his top dresser drawer. There was his box with all the things he brought with him: his penknife, some marbles, the pickle pennies he had earned, and his mother's mother-of-pearl hair comb. The only thing missing was the shooter marble he had given to Laura. He would need to get himself another one when he got to Boston. He tucked his harmonica and the glittery Christmas card from Mistress Renée into the box and then placed it in his sack. He didn't think they would mind if he took his sack; Mrs. Worthington had made it for him for Christmas to carry his books in.

Time to pack some clothes. He would only take the bare necessities, and his jacket of course, the one he wore the night he came. He looked around the room. He needed to write a goodbye note, something so they would not worry. He found a pencil and a piece of paper and started to write:

Dear Worthington Family,
    I am leaving for Boston today. I have tickets from
Mistress Renée. Please do not worry about me. Thank
you for helping me get better and everything you have
done for me. It is time for me to find my own way.

He thought the letter sounded stupid but he couldn't
think of anything else to write, so he signed his name. He
carried the note and his sack into the kitchen. He dropped
the note on the tablecloth next to the lunch Mrs.
Worthington had left for him. He couldn't force one bit of
food down his throat right now. He could go a day without
food. He went to the mudroom to gather up his jacket and
cap. The scarf Laura had made for him hung around the
neck of his jacket. It was the most lopsided scarf he had
ever seen, but he had worn it many times, including when
he fell into the ice pond. He decided to take it with him
since she made it for him. He remembered how excited she
was Christmas morning when she gave it to him. His heart
felt heavy, he would miss her quirkiness and her silly belly
laughs. She was mad at him now. It was better that way,
easier to leave if she was mad.

"Where do you think you're going with your bags all
packed?"

Charley spun around to find himself face to face with
Granny Rozella.

"I am going back to Boston where I belong." Charley
tipped his cap at her and with his sack under his arm and

Laura's scarf tucked in his pocket he half-smiled and said, "Goodbye, Granny, I never did understand why you never liked me. Now you'll be glad that I am gone."

"Good riddance! And you better not be taking anything that doesn't belong to you!"

The door slammed shut harder than Charley had intended. The wind had picked up something fierce. March winds. Laura had told him how they could blow up suddenly and whip you to bits. Charley leaned into the wind. It was coming strong from the north. The sky that had been crystal blue when he was painting now had a menacing gray cast to it. Then he smelled it, that awful choking smell. It made his stomach turn. He hated the smell of smoke. He knew, only too well, what it meant. Charley dropped his sack and ripped off his coat. He sprinted to the barn and flew up the two stories of stairs. Then he scrambled up the ladder that went straight to the top as fast as his legs would go. Sweat was pouring out of him as he reached the top rung. He held on to the sill of the north window of the cupola. There it was! Fire at the Andersons' farm. Even though the farm sat almost a quarter of a mile away, Charley could see that the barn was being consumed by fire. Flames soared high up into the sky, dancing and entwining with one another, increasing their fury. It was a horrible sight. Charley felt dizzy, he was shaking and he could feel the blood rushing to his head. Good Lord, he had to get control of himself! He couldn't pass out now, if he did, he would crash to the floor below.

His nightmare returned to haunt him. The crushing weight of it was unbearable. He fought to push the memory out of his mind. The smell of smoke made him sick. He had smelled it that night. The night that it happened, the night his mother went to Chelsea to help her sister have a baby. His mother often did that; help babies be born. She went and took his little baby brother with her, he was too young to be alone without his mother, she had said. So she took him, and they went to Chelsea and they never came back. The city smelled like burnt rubber for days. The ashes fell all around and no one was allowed to cross the river. No one was allowed in Chelsea. No one ever found them. His mother and brother were just gone, gone to the fire in the big tenement houses. There were too many people to save. The fire grew too fast.

Now Charley screamed. He heard himself scream over and over again. "FIRE! FIRE! FIRE! ANDERSONS' PLACE IS ON FIRE!"

The Worthingtons' barn lay in the direct line of the wind that was gusting stronger by the minute. Charley knew this was big trouble and he had to do something quick. The animals! He had to get the animals out of the barn! He slid down one side of the ladder as if it were a fireman's pole and took the two flights of stairs three at a time. He got Doll, the old mare, out first. He slipped the simple halter over her head and hooked on her lead. She flared her nostrils in fear as he led her from her stall to the outside corral. He slammed the gate tight.

Oh Gawd! The hog had just had piglets and they were in the inside pen. He didn't want a fight with her, she could be one durn ornery pig! He opened the pen to find

that she and her piglets were sleeping soundly. He frantically tied a loop around her neck with a slipknot. Hanging
on the wall was the long pole with a hook that he had seen
Mr. Worthington use to move her. Charley grabbed hold of
it and gave her a good poke. She grunted in irritation and
rolled over. "Come on, ya dumb hog, move it!" He managed to get her up on her feet and then successfully herded
her to the outside pen. Slamming the gate shut he sprinted
back to gather up the piglets; rushing, he scooped up three
in each arm. Two of them wiggled free and fell squealing to
the ground. Charley tossed the four piglets into the outside
pen with their mother and then ran back to catch the two
escapees. They had squirmed themselves over to the corner, one on top of the other. Charley tucked one under
each arm and removed them to the outside pen. Thank
goodness, he didn't have to worry about the mean old male
hog with the sharp tusks; luckily, he was already in an outside pen. And whew, no worry about the cows. They were
safe in the southern pasture.

Charley knew he had to get water quick! His mind flew
through the possibilities. He had to somehow get water to
the roof of the barn. He lined up every pail and bucket he
could find by the pump and then ran to the house for blankets and towels.

"Fire! Fire! The Andersons' barn is on fire! Quick! We
need to get all the blankets we can to douse in water to
cover the roof. Hurry, Granny, the fire is bad and blowing
this way!"

Granny got up from her sewing and marched to the

kitchen window. Charley prayed she would see the hazy smoke billowing, growing closer and closer to them. She squinted her eyes and looked at him with hardened understanding. "Get to the pump boy! I'll get the blankets!"

Charley had pumped several pails full by the time Granny arrived with the blankets. They dipped them in the pails, soaking them in the cold water. "Granny, you keep soaking the blankets while I get these here ones up to the roof. I figure it'll be the first place the sparks will hit. I'll climb to the roof and go through the cupola window!" Charley dragged the dripping blankets, heavy with water, to the barn. He would have to make many trips to cover the roof. He tackled the two flights of stairs with his heavy load. He guessed he wouldn't be able to make it up the upright ladder with the extra weight and keep his balance. He dropped the blankets in a heap on the floor and grabbed two of the dripping blankets. He secured them, one on each shoulder, and then charged up the rungs.

At the top there was a ledge that allowed him a good footing before he went through the window. Just the right amount of leverage was needed to crack the window open. He swatted at the spider webs that tickled his face and got into position. Then he saw them, the nails that had been hammered in before the snows, to keep the windows shut. He yanked with his bare hands at the nail heads that stuck out from the casing. They didn't budge, not one little bit. A hammer, he needed the back of a hammer to pull the nails out. That meant a trip down to the work shed. Dang it, he cussed, precious time wasted. He tucked the wet blankets onto the ledge and catapulted down the ladder, his feet never touching the rungs. He flew down the rest of the stairs and raced into the shed. Perfect! Hanging there on the wall was the tool he needed! The hammer. He tucked it in his belt and ran to the pump.

Granny had soaked more blankets, and had pumped out several more pails. Her arm yanked the pump up and down with relentless determination. Charley loaded up four more blankets, dragging them behind him, creating a soggy trail to the barn. He ascended the stairs with blankets wrapped around his neck and shoulders. At the top he situated himself with a foot astride each side of narrow ledges. He angled himself for the best leverage to pull the nails out. The first one came out easily enough but the second gave him trouble. There was not much of a head for the hammer to grab onto. He locked the prongs of the hammer onto the nail and heaved with all his weight against it. It yielded a small amount, giving him a fraction more nail to work with. After the third wild yank, it released itself completely, almost knocking Charley backwards. Charley regained his position. He laid the hammer on the ledge and with both arms he pushed the bottom casement window up, just like he did in Boston. It opened up enough for him to squeeze himself and a blanket through. He landed on the highest peak of the barn. It was shingled and slippery. He straddled the ridge and inched along carrying the blanket with him. He could see the fire raging on at the Andersons'. A chain of people ran to and

from the pump, sloshing pails of water. He couldn't see
who they were, they were too far away. Charley shuddered.
All their efforts seemed hopeless. The Andersons' barn
was totally consumed by fire.

Charley advanced across the ridge to the far end of the
roof. He spread the blanket out, covering the top of the
ridge, allowing it to hang over the edge by a foot or so.
Going backwards he scooted along the ridge to the window. He retrieved more blankets. Keeping them on his
shoulders, he worked his way along the peak placing the
wet blankets on the north side of the ridge. Four blankets
now covered about a quarter of the roof facing the Andersons'. The wind was unrelenting, sending strong gusts that
thudded into Charley, threatening to push him off balance. Dark clouds covered the sky. Was there any hope for
rain? Charley couldn't stop to think, he made another trip
for wet blankets. Granny had gone through all of the blankets and was now working on whatever she could find;
tablecloths, bedding sheets, quilts, and towels. Rows of
pails, filled to the brim, were waiting for Charley.

"The north side of the barn needs to be watered down!"
Charley yelled as he grabbed two of the pails and flung the
water on the dry barn boards. Granny followed suit, splash-
ing the water as high as her old arms and bent back would
allow her. They didn't speak as they worked; they seemed
to know what to do and acted as a team. The water soaked
into the thirsty planks leaving dark brown stains. When
all the pails were empty, they carried them back to
fill them up again. Granny pumped like an old trooper.

Charley, impressed by her strength, worked hard to keep up with her!

Charley climbed the rungs of the ladder to the top of the barn for what he hoped would be his last time. He had a cramp in his left calf, and his arms and shoulders ached. His muscles weren't as strong as they had been before his accident. He reached the cupola and slid out the window bringing with him as many towels and sheets as he could hoist up and out the window. The top of the barn on the north side was pretty well protected. He couldn't count the number of trips he had already made. He slapped two more down. The weight of the water helped stick them to the roof and hold them in place. Charley noticed, however, that one of the earliest blankets had blown back over on itself exposing some of the wooden shingles. He caught his breath and, for a minute, sat appraising the situation. The Andersons' barn was burnt to a crisp and starting to fall into itself. It was mostly smoke and ashes now. Horrified, Charley watched as the fire leapt to the south side of the house, the side closest to the barn. Several of the men ran into the house, two men dragged out a grandfather clock while others carried arms full of china and precious belongings.

Dead ashes were floating down on him like an early winter snow squall. Charley held his breath and hoped that no live ashes made it across the fields. Then he heard a ghastly sound. An explosion! Glass windows shattered. Fire licked out the broken windows and climbed the walls. The tall oak tree next to the porch ignited like a giant matchstick! Charley watched terrified as flames danced and arched their way across the wooden shingles of the Andersons' roof.

Determined not to let the barn catch fire, Charley decided he would make yet another trip down for wet blankets. The one that had blown over needed to be replaced. His lungs rebelled. He had taken in a lot of smoke. He started to cough and hack as he crawled back to the cupola's window. He had to stop and catch his breath. Oh, what he wouldn't do for a cold drink of water. That's when he saw it, the edge of a wooden shingle that was lit up like a hot coal. The wind dropped it smack on the front side of the barn's roof. It sizzled and smoldered in the moisture of the blanket. Charley didn't want to take any chances, he wrapped a wet towel around his neck and shimmied himself over the ridge and down the slanted pitch of the roof. He kept his body flat against the shingles, his fingers holding on to the tiny edges. His leg was cramping badly, his toes searched blindly below him hoping to find one of the ice clips. He remembered that they were spaced alternately on the roof to secure the heavy snow and ice in winter from creating an avalanche. He had to find one now to prevent himself from sliding off the roof. Ah, there it was, partially covered by a wet blanket. He pushed the blanket away with the tip of his toe and placed the heavy sole of his boot firmly against it.

Now, only a matter of inches from the burning shingle, he stretched his arm and fingers out as far as he could. His hand seized the angry red ember. The heat seared right through his skin. He released it, wincing in pain. Charley's heart was pounding in his ears. He stretched to pick it up! This time he secured it with the corner of a wet towel. He slapped the ends over it so no air could possibly fan it alive. Holding on to the ember in the towel, he climbed like a lizard on his belly to the top ridge. He pulled himself onto it with his one free hand. Then he threw one leg over the top, straddling it. He cussed himself for being stupid enough to pick up a burning ember with his bare hands.

He stayed straddled on the roof. It was getting hard to see, the sky was darkened with smoke. His eyes smarted from it. He heard thunder rumbling in the distance. Would rain save the barn? Thunder also meant lightening. And here he sat, perched on top of the roof, like a lightning rod!

Exhaustion was getting the better of him; maybe he should leave his post, get some more towels and check on Granny. He looked over at the Andersons'. It was a sore sight. The house looked too far-gone to save. Whatever exploded had caused the fire to run its full course. Just then, a red flaming rocket flew past him like fireworks on the Fourth of July! He twisted himself around to see where it landed. The far side of the barn was uncovered. He watched as the ignited ember hit the roof. It landed snug, in a crack, between two shingles.

Charley, with more willpower than he knew he possessed, slid the last wet towel around his neck; then standing up and desperately hanging on to the edge of the cupola's roof, he inched his way around to the backside. He could smell it, the burning ember, like the beginnings of an innocent campfire. He slid his leg over the ridge, straddling the roof's peak. He then lowered himself on his belly down the incline of the roof. The red-hot ember was just beyond his grasp. His brain was tired. What could he do? Maybe he could throw the towel and try to cover it. But, if he missed, the ember could slide down onto the roof of the tool shed directly below or—even worse—the fresh pile of hay stacked next to it. He could not risk it. He slid down a few more inches. The toe of his boot found a metal ice clip. He whistled through his teeth and braced himself. He could do it! He wrapped the towel around his hand like a mitt and reached for the burning ember. There were black burn marks already forming on either side of it. He stretched his arm, straining every muscle. All the while, he kept himself flat as a pancake, balancing all his weight on one leg.

Hallelujah! He got it! The heat of the ember sizzled against the wet towel. He started to regain his position when his foot slid off the ice clip as suddenly as if he had stepped on a banana peel. One hand held onto the towel and the other grasped for anything to prevent his fall. He rolled like a limp rag doll, landing square on the roof of the adjacent tool shed. The tool shed slanted at an even steeper slope, sending Charley downwards like a spinning top. The next thing he knew he was flat on his back on top of the pile of hay.

Granny Rozella, with black skirts flapping, rushed to his side. "Are you all right, boy? Can you move your legs and arms?" The wind had been knocked out of him. The sky spun around above his head. He sat up slowly, bracing himself with his left arm. He felt as if he were riding on a merry-go-round that wouldn't stop. His stomach lurched; he leaned to the side to throw up. Once he emptied his stomach, he found the dizziness eased. Cool raindrops drizzled down on his face. Granny helped hoist him to his feet. With him leaning on her, the two hobbled back to the house. Under his arm, wrapped in a wet towel, Charley carried the remains of the burnt ember.

CHAPTER 21

Coming Home

Granny busied herself with cleaning Charley's burnt hand. "It will sting a little from the alcohol, but we got to get this clean or it will get infected." The alcohol smelled sharp and acrid in his sore nose as she poured it on the clean cloth and dabbed at his hand. "This is a mean burn you got here. It will take some time to heal."

The alcohol stung like a wasp. He pulled his hand away. "Sorry, Granny! It stings!"

Charley heard the clomping of the horses' hooves. He looked around the table wildly. Where was his letter to the Worthingtons? The lunch, he never ate, sat alone on the table. There was no trace of his note. He had to get it back. He didn't want them to see it. And where was his sack with his box? He had lost all track of it with the fire. Charley panicked. He bent over to see if the note had fallen under the table.

"No need to worry about that letter you wrote. I threw it away."

"You did? But why?" Charley hesitated, and then asked again, "Why did you throw it away, Granny? Didn't you want me to go?"

She stopped fussing about him and looked him straight in the eye. "Never mind about that. A body has a right to change her mind. And if you're looking for your sack, it is in your room where it belongs." Was he imagining things? It was as if . . . "Now hold still and let me clean all this nasty dirt and smoke off your face."

Bam! The door slammed! Mr. Worthington, covered in smoke and sweat, strode into the kitchen. Laura and Lynette, tired and bedraggled, followed him. Mrs. Worthington, holding Lana's hand as she toddled, entered last. They all looked smoke stained and utterly exhausted. The only one missing was Harlan. They all stood in a semi-circle staring down at Charley.

Mr. Worthington addressed him, "The Andersons' farm is gone. We did all we could do to save it. We were on our way into town when we passed some folks who told us the Andersons' place was on fire. Folks came from all the farms to help. We did everything we could, but we couldn't stop it; the blaze had caught on too strong. It's a shame to see a good farm go." He dropped down hard onto the kitchen chair. Charley never saw him like this; Mr. Worthington was all choked up. Then he turned toward Charley and said, "Didn't you smell the smoke, boy? Couldn't you see the flames? Why didn't you come to help? That is what neighbors do here; they help each other."

The lump in Charley's throat stopped him from answering.

"But Pa!" Laura piped up. "Charley looks as terrible as we do. Look! His clothes are full of smoke and are stained wet-dirty just like ours."

Harlan stormed through the mudroom door and skidded into the kitchen. He looked like he had seen a ghost. "Someone's been on the roof of the barn; there are blankets and quilts thrown all over the side that faces the Andersons'. The whole north side of the barn has been soaked down too! I seen it when I put the horses away. And old Doll, the mare, is outside in the corral and the ma hog is in the outside pen with her squealers!"

"Are you all daft?" demanded Granny. "Charley looks like he does because he sure enough saved our farm! Can't you see the boy is near worn to his death? He has been up on the roof of the barn all day puttin' down the wet blankets. He has terrible burns on his hands from catching flying embers. He rolled off of the roof, nearly breaking his back, to catch the last ember before the rain. Yes sir, you can all be thankful to this boy. For today he saved our blessed farm!"

The whole room was frozen in time.

Mrs. Worthington broke the silence; she put baby Lana in her play box and threw her arms around Charley's neck rocking him back and forth. "Thank you, Charley, thank you my dear, dear, boy. We were all so caught up in the poor Andersons' plight that none of us gave a thought of the fire spreading to our farm!"

Mr. Worthington pushed himself from the table and stood towering over Charley. He took a deep breath before he spoke. "First, son, I guess I owe you an apology, and second, I would like to thank you for saving our farm." He reached his hand out to shake Charley's hand but when he saw the badly burned hand he put his hand on Charley's

shoulder and looked him straight in the eye. He pulled a
letter out of his pocket. "I had a letter written to Reverend
Matthews to be delivered to the post office today. You
didn't appear to be happy here, so I wrote to him that it
would be best for you to return to the Home. It never got
mailed because of the fire." He took the letter and put it on
the table in front of Charley. "I do not wish to mail this
letter now. Instead I am asking you, Charley, to think
about if you are willing to continue to stay with us and be
a part of our family here on the farm?"

"Well sir, I . . . I . . ."

Laura interrupted, wiping her tear-splashed eyes with
her sleeve, making smudges across her face. "We want you
to stay, Charley! Oh, please stay! We would miss you, too
terribly much, if you went away. Don't go back to the
Home!" Laura looked pleadingly at Charley.

Lynette, clinging to Laura and sobbing, managed to
squeak out a sad little, "Please stay, Charley."

Harlan cleared his throat, "Charley, I would like to
shake your hand 'cause what you did today was good. But I
see you hurt it bad, so I can't." Harlan scuffed the sole of
his boot across the wooden floor. "I tried to save you when
you fell in the ice pond, I didn't mean for you to fall in.
Sorry I hit you in the head with the tongs. And I know
you thought it was me that wrecked your red coat . . ."

Granny bristled, "Okay, that's enough. Let the poor
boy get some food in him, he hasn't eaten all day."

Charley sputtered, "Mr. Worthington, sir, I, um . . . I'm
glad I was able to stop the fire and save the barn."

"I am glad too, son, now let the women get some food in you." Mr. Worthington placed his hat on his head and started for the door. "Come on, Harlan, we'd best be getting the ladies in from the pasture, 'fore it's past their time." Charley grinned from ear to ear. He was starving! He was hungry enough to eat a whole cow!

Laura bounced into the dining room. She had on a new blue taffeta dress with pink rosebuds that Granny had made for her. She wore her hair unbraided with finger curls that dangled halfway down her back. A blue velvet ribbon that matched the color of her dress was tied in a neat bow on top of her head. Her brown eyes danced with excitement. Charley smiled. Laura was the only person he knew who could charge a whole room with energy all by herself. Laura inspected her richly decorated birthday cake. With a flip of her finger she sliced one of the iced flowers from the border and plopped it greedily into her mouth.

"Laura Ann, now that you are ten years old you are expected to be a lady!" Mrs. Worthington scolded as she entered the dining room carrying a tray full of plates, cups and saucers. She stacked the dishes on the table, humming to herself as she returned to the kitchen.

"Laura, I have a present for you. Would you like to open it now?" Charley felt bashful, but he wanted her to open his present.

"Why surely, Charley, I would love to open a present

from you! Are ya hidin' it?" Laura's face was full of delightful anticipation.

Charley whipped his hand out from behind him and
presented Laura with a box wrapped in brown paper and
tied with a lace ribbon.

"Happy birthday, Laura!"

Laura accepted the present eagerly. Her eyes were as
wide as the saucers on the table. "Thank you, Charley. It's
so pretty! I hardly want to open it!"

"Go ahead, you can open it! Granny gave me the ribbon to wrap it up all pretty for you." Charley was eager for
her to open it while they were alone.

Laura grinned at Charley and tugged one end of the
ribbon, teasing it to come undone. It slid easily away from
the package. She laid the ribbon with care on the table
and began to slowly unwrap the paper. Charley thought it
was taking her forever to open it. He was anxious to see if
she would like it or not!

As the paper fell to the floor, Laura stared at the box.
It was an ordinary box with nothing fancy inscribed on it.
She popped the top off and peaked inside. She gasped.
Tears welled up in her eyes, her impish grin gone. Charley's
heart plummeted like a dead weight to his feet. He had
hoped that she would like it. Bewildered and disappointed,
he stood there before her feeling like a fool. Then, without
any forewarning, she threw her arms around his neck and
hugged him so hard he almost toppled over.

She exclaimed as she released him, "Oh my! Charley!
Thank you so much! It is so very beautiful. Oh, I know

how much it meant to you. I promise I will treasure it forever and always!"

Charley whispered, "I wanted you to have it."

"But Charley, it was your mother's, your mother's hair comb! Are you sure you want me to have it?" Before Charley could answer, Laura had ripped the ribbon out of her hair and had tucked the mother-of-pearl hair comb into her curls. She spun around for Charley to admire. The afternoon's sun caught the comb in its rays. It glistened as if it were made of pure gold.

"The comb sure looks pretty in your hair, Laura. It has found its home!"

"And you too, Charley! You have found your home too!"

"Yes, Laura, I have!"

Epilogue

DEAR READER, if you are like me, you will be yearning to know the rest of Charley's story.

So here it is in a nutshell! Charley stayed on the farm, worked hard, and became adept at his farm chores. Charley found his new family, but always kept his sister and brothers in his heart.

Clarence was unhappy and ran away from the farm in western Massachusetts. He found his way to Greene, Maine, and the front door of the Worthingtons' farm. Mrs. Worthington welcomed him with open arms. Clarence pitched in and did his share of the work, but he never did become a farmer. Minnie and George remained in contact with Clarence and Charley, and over the years they made many visits to the farm. They stayed in touch for the rest of their lives.

When Laura reached high school age, she was sent to live with her aunt and uncle in Lewiston, Maine. She completed her four years of high school there, while Charley worked on the farm as well as doing other odd jobs to earn money. Charley saved every penny to buy a farm of his own. After Charley had saved one thousand dollars, he asked for Laura's hand in marriage. The Worthingtons gave them their blessings and Laura and Charley were happily married. They bought a small farm nearby and raised a family. The family has grown from children, to grandchildren, great-grandchildren and now one great-great-grandchild and many more greats in the generations to come!

Background Sources

IT WAS AFTER a charming summer's eve picnic dinner, when my dear friend and neighbor stacked up his knife, fork and spoon on his plate. I watched as he did this, intrigued, and then asked him why.

He answered with a twinkle in his eye, "My father did that after every meal! He learned to do that at the New England Home for Little Wanderers. When you live in an orphanage it is easier to clear the table that way! One grab, and *whoosh* the silverware is all gone." That was the beginning of the Charley stories! My friend, over many meetings, relayed one sad or delightful tale after another. "My father could sing, he had the voice of an angel," he told me. Eagerly, I wrote each and every wonderful vignette down. I had become more than intrigued; I had fallen in love with Charley.

My friend's older brother came to visit and heartily joined in with Charley stories; soon stories were pouring in from sisters and other family members. My neighbor's sister found a swatch of Charley's tweed coat and lining; on it was pinned a note, "the coat that Charley wore the night he came to Maine." My friend loaned me the cut piece to have by my side to inspire me if I should need it along the way!

I was hungry for more Charley research. Being a visual person as well as a sleuth, my husband and I packed the car and headed up to Greene, Maine. We found the train station that Charley and the choir arrived at, and the Baptist

Church, directly across from the station, where Charley sang his last solo with the choir. Our final goal was to locate the family farm. I called my neighbor on my cell phone and, standing there on a farm, I described it to him. "Yes, that's it; you found it!"

On a hunch, I decided to see if I could find anything written about the New England Home for Little Wanderers, and to my delight I found *The History of The New England Home for Little Wanderers* written by Roberta Star Hirshson in collaboration with Clifford W. Falby. It verified all that I had been told. There was a choir, and it was renowned for its beautiful voices. In the Boston Public Library, I looked up on old microfiche tapes the 1910 editions of the *Boston Daily Globe*. There I found proof of the choir, with advertisements placed announcing dates and times of concerts performed by the New England Home's children's choir.

Having personal experience with children who are in desperate need of finding a family of their own, I could relate to the inner feelings of a child who suffers from being unable to be placed in a family. I am a former childcare worker and teacher at the very same New England Home for Little Wanderers. As a matter of fact, that is where I met my husband, a former childcare worker, as well. During the years we worked there it was no longer an orphanage; it had become a residential treatment center for emotionally disturbed children.

Not being a farmer myself, I needed more farming information, particularly during the early 1900s, so a visit to the New Hampshire Farm Museum was in order. The interior of the house and the farming tools were all there. Ice cutting was something I needed to learn more about. Luck was with me, an ice cutting demonstration was being held at Sturbridge Village Museum, so my husband and I drove to Sturbridge, Massachusetts, and learned to cut blocks of ice out of a frozen lake.

Now, I readily admit I am not at all crazy about heights, but after asking permission, I climbed to the top of my near neighbor's barn. It sported a peaked roof and cupola, just like the Worthingtons'. I made it to the top, my stomach rebelling every step up the ladder, but, boy-oh-boy, now I could feel and write about how Charley would feel way up there!

I needed to research what chores a farm boy would do during that time in history. I searched the Internet and found an absolutely delightful book, *Bob Artly's Book of Farm Chores, As Remembered by a Former Kid*, Voyageur Press, Inc., 2002. This book became my bible for Charley's farm chores! Bob Artly also has written *Bob Artly's Seasons of the Farm*, Voyageur Press, Inc., 2002.

Much drier—but packed full of information on homeless children of this time—is a book by Peter C. Holloran: *Boston's Wayward Children, Social Services for Homeless Children*. 1830–1930, Northeastern University Press edition, 1994.

This novel is based on oral accounts and family memories, along with my research. Some names have been changed. *Charley*, the novel, is a work of historical fiction.

About the Author

CHARLEY is award-winning author Donna Seim's second novel for eight to twelve-year-olds and her first historical fiction. *Hurricane Mia*, her first novel, tells an adventure story set in the Caribbean.

Donna is also the author of the picture books *Satchi and Little Star* and *Where is Simon, Sandy?* *Satchi and Little Star* is a three-time award-winning picture book about an island girl, Satchi, who tries to catch and tame a wild horse for her very own. *Where is Simon, Sandy?*, Donna's first picture book, is a two-time national-award-winning story based on a true tale about a little donkey that wouldn't quit.

Donna is a graduate from The Ohio State University with a BSSW in the field of social welfare. Donna also holds a MA in Special Education from Lesley University. She is a member of the Society of Children's Book Writers & Illustrators.

Donna lives in Newbury, Massachusetts, with her husband, Martin, and her dog, Rags. You can see more of her work at www.donnaseim.com.

About the Illustrator

SUSAN SPELLMAN pursues a dual career as a fine artist and as an illustrator with extensive experience in painting, portraiture, and children's book illustration. Her work can be viewed at: www.suespellmanstudio.com.

Her fine art work can be viewed at: www.spellman collection.com.